SWEET YULETIDE

Indigo Bay Christmas Romances
Book Four

Melissa McClone

Sweet Yuletide
Indigo Bay Christmas Romances (Book 4)
Copyright © 2020 Melissa McClone

ALL RIGHT RESERVED

Cover by Najla Qamber Designs
www.najlaqamberdesigns.com

Cardinal Press, LLC
October 2020
ISBN-13: 9781944777500

INDIGO BAY CHRISTMAS ROMANCES

What is the Indigo Bay Christmas Romances series? It's a continuation of the popular Indigo Bay Sweet Romance and Second Chance Romance series with tons of fun for readers! But more specifically, it's a set of books written by authors who love romance. Grab a mug of hot chocolate, drop into a comfy chair, and get ready to be swept away into this charming South Carolina beach town.

The Indigo Bay world has been written so readers can dive in anywhere in the series without missing a beat. Read one or all—they're all sweet, fun rides that you won't soon forget. Also, as special treats, you'll see some recurring characters. How many can you find?

Indigo Bay Christmas Romances
Sweet Tidings (Book 1) by Jean C. Gordon
Sweet Noel (Book 2) by Jeanette Lewis
Sweet Joymaker (Book 3) by Jean Oram
Sweet Yuletide (Book 4) by Melissa McClone
Sweet Mistletoe (Book 5) by Elizabeth Bromke
Sweet Carol (Book 6) by Shanae Johnson

Indigo Bay Second Chance Romances
Sweet Troublemaker (Book 1) by Jean Oram
Sweet Do-Over (Book 2) by Melissa McClone
Sweet Horizons (Book 3) by Jean C. Gordon

Sweet Complications (Book 4) by Stacy Claflin
Sweet Whispers (Book 5) by Jeanette Lewis
Sweet Adventure (Book 6) by Tamie Dearen

Indigo Bay Sweet Romance Series
Sweet Dreams (Book 1) by Stacy Claflin
Sweet Matchmaker (Book 2) by Jean Oram
Sweet Sunrise (Book 3) by Kay Correll
Sweet Illusions (Book 4) by Jeanette Lewis
Sweet Regrets (Book 5) by Jennifer Peel
Sweet Rendezvous (Book 6) by Danielle Stewart
Sweet Saturdays (Book 7) by Pamela Kelley
Sweet Beginnings (Book 8) by Melissa McClone
Sweet Starlight (Book 9) by Kay Correll
Sweet Forgiveness (Book 10) by Jean Oram
Sweet Reunion (Book 11) by Stacy Claflin
Sweet Entanglement (Book 12) by Jean C. Gordon

Holiday Short Reads
Sweet Holiday Surprise by Jean Oram
Sweet Holiday Memories by Kay Correll
Sweet Holiday Wishes by Melissa McClone
Sweet Holiday Traditions by Danielle Stewart

Missing some books from your collection?

Find out more about Indigo Bay at
www.sweetreadbooks.com/indigo-bay

DEDICATION

For all the readers who fell in love
with Indigo Bay the way I did.

1

Instrumental Christmas music played in the Berry Lake Art Gallery, but Sheridan DeMarco wasn't in the mood for hearing holiday tunes. The tasteful décor—white lights and a miniature tree with gold and silver bell ornaments—was bad enough. She hadn't meant to get her Grinch on or channel Ebenezer Scrooge, but it had happened anyway.

That was a bummer because she loved Christmas. Rather, she used to love it. But after leaving in the middle of Thanksgiving dinner two days ago, the thought of all the family gatherings associated with December twenty-fifth made her want to break out in hives, especially not knowing what her future held.

Don't think about it.

She focused on dusting a large Bigfoot

sculpture. The fierce-looking Sasquatch stood on a pedestal in an alcove. The out-of-the-way spot kept tourists from blocking the artwork for sale. Her small town—okay, the local business association her father belonged to—touted the figurine as one of the top-ten photo ops in Berry Lake, Washington. That brought in plenty of customers, but poor Squatchy—as nicknamed by locals—needed constant cleaning from the people touching it.

Job security, her dad had once joked.

If only that were still true.

A weight pressed down on her shoulders, joining the imaginary band that had been tightening inch by inch around her chest since Thanksgiving night.

She shook it off.

Well, she tried to shake it off.

Sheridan polished the thumbprints from Bigfoot's eyes. "At least my dad won't fire *you*."

No matter how many times she'd told herself not to obsess about her job, she couldn't stop thinking about it. If not consciously, then subconsciously, because a boulder occupied the pit of her stomach. Worry, fear, and disbelief had kept her awake for the past two nights. Would tonight be any different?

Part of her didn't want to know the answer.

The Berry Lake Gallery was Sal DeMarco's pride and joy, and where Sheridan had grown up.

This shop on Main Street was the only home she had left since her parents' divorce. She knew every inch of the building, including her apartment upstairs, and loved art as much as her dad did. He'd said—*promised*—she would take over when he retired. But now...

A bone-chilling cold prickled her skin.

Perhaps what happened at Thanksgiving dinner had been a big misunderstanding. And maybe Santa would bring her the perfect boyfriend for Christmas, too.

Who am I kidding?

Thursday night with her dad and his new family had been a living nightmare. The only question was how badly the fallout would affect her.

The bell over the door jingled, and her father stepped inside. His hair used to be gray at the temples, which made him look distinguished and more handsome, but her stepmother, Deena, demanded he dye his hair for their wedding last month. He wore slacks and a leather jacket—his going-out-to-dinner clothes—something he did regularly since he'd remarried.

He flipped the Open sign to Closed.

Uh-oh.

As Sheridan's muscles tightened, she gripped the dust cloth.

He never closed the gallery early unless it was an emergency. "Emergency" defined as going to the hospital or needing the fire department. Then again, her father hadn't acted like himself since Deena entered his life. Sheridan wanted to tell herself this wasn't a big deal, but everything inside her said one thing...

It's time.

After Sheridan walked out in the middle of Thanksgiving dinner, she'd been waiting to hear from him, but he hadn't called, texted, or stopped by the gallery yesterday—Black Friday, one of their busiest days of the year.

Is life as I know it over with?

She shivered.

When her once-stable life was ripped apart by the two people she loved most in the world, the gallery became Sheridan's sanctuary and salvation. She'd believed nothing worse could ever happen to her than her parents' divorce. But both of them remarrying within weeks of each other had proven otherwise. She'd gone from being an only child to having four stepsiblings with her dad's new family and three with her mom's. Growing pains didn't come close to describing the issues with the two blended families this past month. But surely, Deena and her kids hadn't replaced Sheridan in her father's heart.

He went behind the counter, sat on the stool, and typed on the computer's keyboard. "You sold more than I thought you would yesterday."

With a pat on Bigfoot's belly for luck, she joined her father in the central area of the gallery.

"Profits are up twenty-five percent this month because I've been doing my job." Which was why she had to ask, "Is it still mine, or is Remy replacing me?"

During dinner the other night, her stepsister had begged to work full-time at the gallery. Deena had praised her daughter and dissed Sheridan. So had Ian, Deena's youngest son. Then, Owen, Remy's twin, had offered his small-business experience to take the gallery to the next level, as if Sheridan had no idea what she was doing. Thank goodness the oldest son, Dalton, hadn't been there or she might have taken more verbal abuse.

Her dad had said nothing, but Sheridan hadn't been able to take the insults from his new family, so she'd risen from the table, grabbed her jacket and purse, and left. But his silence wouldn't do now.

"You can't afford to pay both of us." She wouldn't go another hour without an answer. "And what experience does Owen offer when he's clueless about art and how galleries operate?"

Her father dragged his hand through his hair. "Please understand. I'm in a tough spot."

"Answer the question." She wouldn't let him play the victim. "Are you replacing me with Remy?"

Her dad didn't meet Sheridan's gaze. "Yes."

The word sliced her heart in half. She struggled to breathe.

"Why?" Sheridan hated how weak she sounded, but she'd hoped—prayed—her father would stand up to Deena this time and put his daughter first. Something he hadn't done since he'd fallen in love. "The gallery means everything to me. All I've ever wanted to do is work with you here. I've put my heart and soul into making it a success. You've never once complained about my work."

"This is important to my wife."

Sheridan nearly laughed. "I'm your daughter. You promised the gallery would be mine someday."

Guilt flashed across his face. "Deena thinks Owen is better suited to run it."

Sheridan's breath hitched. "You promised, Dad."

"Deena thinks Remy will thrive here."

One more "Deena thinks," and I'll scream. She also noticed he hadn't mentioned his promise.

Tears burned her eyes, but she blinked them away.

Ever since the wedding last month, his new family had treated her as if she belonged in the recycle bin. She'd kept waiting for her dad to stand up for her. Now, she realized that had been a pipe dream. "So, your daughter is out, and your stepdaughter is in."

Her father's mouth thinned. "That's not fair."

"Don't talk to me about fair. You're taking away the only thing that matters to me because someone who wasn't a part of your life four months ago says it's a good idea. When you told me you were marrying Deena, I supported you because she seemed to make you happy. When she wanted her kids to be the only wedding party members, I didn't say a word, even though there was space for another bridesmaid to even out the numbers. But Deena's turned into a caricature of an evil stepmother, and you're playing right along. She's been widowed once and divorced twice. With each marriage, she adds to her net worth. Have you considered she wants her kids to work here so they can run the gallery once it belongs to her?"

As his expression hardened, the lines on his face deepened. "What a horrible, spiteful thing to say. I'm so disappointed in you. Deena was right when she called you a spoiled brat, an only child who's been handed everything. It's time you see how easy you've had it all these years."

His words struck with the force of cannonballs. It was all Sheridan could do not to take a step backward and retreat. He sounded nothing like the man who'd wiped her tears, bandaged her knees, taught her everything about art, and taken her on trips to museums around the world. The man in front of her had become unrecognizable. All that mattered to him now was Deena and her children.

"Remy wants to live in the apartment upstairs," he said. "You need to be out by December first."

Sheridan's jaw dropped. "That's only three days away."

"Then you'd better start packing. Deena said—"

"Forget your wife." Sheridan balled her fist. "Your daughter is standing right in front of you. Your only daughter, who is now jobless and will be homeless in three days. Your daughter, who has worked at your side for years to make this gallery what it is today. Doesn't that mean anything to you? Don't *I* mean anything?"

"Deena said this would be good for you. Starting Monday, you'll train Remy. It shouldn't take long. She's a smart young woman. Then you can find another job."

Unbelievable. Sheridan hadn't gained two families with her parents' marriages. She'd lost her father.

His choice.

The wrong one, which she hoped he realized before he lost everything because of Deena.

That didn't make Sheridan feel any better, but something else would. While her father remained seated, she grabbed her purse and coat from the back room before removing the keys to the gallery. She handed them to her dad. "Here you go."

"Keys?"

"I quit."

"I need you to train—"

"I won't." Sheridan shrugged on her coat. "You've made it clear your new family is more important than your old one. You want Remy here. You train her."

"Don't do this, Sheridan. I'm your father."

"Not any longer." She half laughed. That was better than crying. "A father who loves his daughter would never do this to her. I'll be out of the apartment on the thirtieth. The keys will be on the kitchen counter, Sal."

He flinched. "You're so much like your mother."

"Since it appears I only have one parent who cares about me, I'll take that as a compliment."

With her shoulders pushed back and her head held high, Sheridan walked out the front entrance, wondering if she would ever step foot in the gallery again. She went around the building and climbed the stairs to her apartment. At least it was hers for three more days.

Hand trembling, she inserted the key in the lock and opened the door.

The smell of home—vanilla and sandalwood leftover from candles she'd lit last night—wrapped around her like a fleece blanket, soft and warm. As soon as she placed her purse on a hook, her phone rang. The ringtone of dog barks belonged to her mom.

"Hey." Sheridan didn't try to sound anything other than defeated.

"Please tell me your father didn't fire and evict

you." Her mother's words tumbled out like one of the spring-fed waterfalls that flowed into Berry Lake.

In a small town, news traveled like wildfire, but this was speed-of-light fast. Sheridan gripped her phone. "Who told you?"

"I bumped into Deena at the cupcake shop. She suggested I clear out a bedroom and have a job for you at the rescue because Sal was hiring Remy to take your place and giving her the apartment. Then she really gloated, saying Owen would be the new gallery manager." If eye-rolling had a voice, it would sound like Sabine Culpepper. "That woman must rub dollar bills all over her body to keep from smelling like a wannabe. Her children aren't any better."

Maybe worse. "I only know Owen, Remy, and Ian. Dalton didn't attend the wedding or come home for Thanksgiving."

"He's older than you, so you probably don't remember him. He's more like his father Paul than the other three kids, who take after their mother. I haven't seen him since he graduated high school and left Berry Lake. But enough about the Dwyer family." Her mom's voice softened. "I'm so sorry, honey. I know how much the gallery means to you."

Sheridan struggled to breathe. "I don't understand how a father could do this to his daughter."

"Deena has him wrapped around her finger."

"But I'm his daughter." Sheridan thought he loved her. She blinked back tears. "I've lost my job, my apartment, and my father because of her. They hardly know each other."

"It sucks, baby. And the worst part, Deena has done this same thing before, but men assume they'll be different until they aren't. I'm dumbfounded your dad fell for it."

"He expected me to train Remy."

Her mother swore under her breath. "What did you say?"

"Nothing. I quit, handed over my keys to the gallery, and walked out."

"That's my girl."

She sniffled. "He said I was like you."

"You're the best parts of us both. Your father will wake up one day and realize his mistakes, but the damage is done, and I have no doubt the gallery will eventually belong to Deena and her minions. I'm just sorry he's hurt you so badly."

Sheridan was sorry, too. She plopped onto her overstuffed couch. "What am I supposed to do now?"

"Move in here. Max won't mind. I can't pay you, but you can volunteer at the rescue. Oh, the cupcake shop has a Help Wanted sign in the window. You've worked with Missy Hanford at cat adoption events. She'll put in a good word for you with Elise Landon."

"Thanks. I won't get a recommendation from the gallery." Which was Sheridan's only work experience unless she counted the volunteer hours at the animal rescue. "I'll make a résumé tonight and take it to the cupcake shop on Monday morning."

"I'll be over tomorrow with boxes to help you pack. It might take a few trips with Max's truck, but we'll get it done."

Sheridan glanced around her apartment, imagining her Christmas tree in its usual corner. That wouldn't happen this year. No lights would hang in the window, either. As her chest tightened, she blew out a breath. "Okay."

"It'll work out. Trust your mama."

"I'm trying." But first, Sheridan needed to have a good cry. "I love you, Mom."

2

Sunday was the weekly family dinner, not Tuesday night. That hadn't stopped Michael Patterson from jumping at his mom's invitation. A second home-cooked meal in three days was worth driving through Charleston's rush-hour traffic. For over a month, he'd bounced from one friend's place to another. Eating fast food, takeout, and pizza was getting old. Besides, he wanted to see his parents before he left town for the rest of December.

Michael opened the front door, not bothering to knock. He'd grown up in this house with his brother and two sisters. After he stepped inside, he closed the door.

The sharp pine scent from the decorated tree in the corner and the faint smell of smoke from the wood burning in the fireplace hung on the air. Only

Christmas carols were missing. Not hearing the music was strange. His mom played them nonstop until December twenty-sixth.

As he entered the living room, Michael froze, surprised to see all his family. They sat on the two couches and chairs: his mom and dad; Mason, Ashleigh, and baby Monroe; Madison and Rory; and Marley and Von.

Michael hadn't expected his parents to invite his three siblings and their significant others. That never happened during the week, but maybe his mom was trying out a new recipe and wanted everyone's opinion. It wasn't a problem. The Patterson family motto was *the more, the merrier*. This would save him from texting each of his siblings about going out of town for Christmas.

With a grin, he adjusted his baseball cap. "If I'd known everyone would be here, I would have worn something other than sweats and a hoodie."

A joke, because he'd worn that most days since he'd lost his job.

No one laughed or smiled.

Weird. His family looked like wax figures from that tourist attraction up north.

Unease trickled along his spine. "Everything okay?"

His dad motioned to an empty chair. "Take a seat, Mikey."

He'd been Mikey for as long as he could

remember, but the nickname bristled. Still, it beat "big baby" or "big boy." Even though he was the youngest of the four kids, his siblings called him their "big" brother because of his six-foot-three height and broad shoulders. His athletic build had come in handy playing sports through college, and he still enjoyed working out. It also paid off because dressing up like a superhero for Halloween made all the pretty ladies want to flirt and take selfies with him and his shield.

As Michael sat, he glanced at the clock on the wall.

I'm not late.

So why was everyone staring at him like he wore two different shoes? A glance at his feet showed they were the same, but his socks were different colors.

No one spoke, but they kept looking at him.

"Seriously, guys. You're freaking me out." He rubbed the back of his neck. "What's going on?"

Baby Monroe slept soundly in Mason's arms and appeared fine. No one looked sick or injured. Yet they remained silent.

"Mom?"

His mother fingered the edges of her apron. Something she did only when nervous. She inhaled deeply before exhaling. "Have you found a new job?"

Oh, great. The stop-messing-up-your-life lecture

was coming. Again. He guessed the weekly "you're a loser" talks weren't enough for them. "No."

Which they should have known since they'd discussed this on Sunday night—forty-eight hours ago.

His dad crossed his arms. "You'll have to explain the gap in your resume."

Michael swallowed a sigh. This had to be the hundredth time he'd said this, but he would say it again. "The company went under. It isn't my fault I lost my job."

He wished his family understood that. Instead, they viewed him as Mikey, the twenty-seven-year-old man-child who partied too much on weekends and lost his job when the start-up he'd worked at for three years folded. He'd loved his position in the marketing department. He'd been promoted twice and, on occasion, helped code, too. But the founders—two tech guys—had mismanaged everything so badly the investors had salvaged what they could before walking away.

Being unemployed, however, had been a blessing. Just one he couldn't share with anyone.

Yet.

Still, he needed to tell his family something, even if it wasn't what they wanted to hear.

"I'm keeping my eyes open." Not a lie. Occasionally, he checked the job listings online and thanked his lucky stars he would never work for someone else again. "Trust me. Everything will turn around in the new year."

"Have you found a place to live?" Mason asked.

"Not yet." Michael hadn't renewed his lease. Extreme, perhaps, but he didn't want to raise suspicions if he wanted a different place in January. Not having a job had given him the perfect excuse to move out. "I'm staying with Tristan."

For now.

Madison's eyebrows knotted. "I thought you were over at Isaac's?"

"That was last week."

"What about Brendan?" Rory asked.

Marley's mouth quirked. "You were at Colton's for a few days."

The shared glances flying around the room made Michael's hands clammy. He rubbed them against his sweats. "I've stayed with each one of them."

His father brushed his hand through his salt-and-pepper hair. "Aren't you a little old to be couch-surfing?"

Michael fought the urge to roll his eyes. "It's temporary, Dad. If you're worried about my living situation—"

"We're worried about you, Mikey." The words rushed out of Marley's mouth.

Von held her hand but said nothing.

Ashleigh nodded.

Madison leaned forward. "You were laid off in September, and you still don't have a job. Rory offered you one, and so did Von."

"I thanked them, but those jobs weren't right for me." Michael envisioned his perfect life. Soon, it would be his. "As I said, things will turn around in the new year."

And in a big way.

One day, he'd been laid off, handed a lousy severance package, and escorted out of the building with his personal belongings in a box that had once held copier paper. The following afternoon, when he normally would have been at work, he'd bought a candy bar and a lottery ticket at a corner convenience market. That night, his ticket not only matched all the numbers, but it was also the only winner of a seven-hundred-million-dollar jackpot.

Unbelievable but true.

Now accountants, financial planners, and attorneys worked for him. Fortunately, he could claim his prize anonymously since he lived in South Carolina, but his team was doing the legwork so no one could track the money to him. A trust was involved, maybe two, because he wanted to make sure his family, especially sweet little Monroe and any future nieces and nephews, were safe from kidnappers and whoever else preyed on the wealthy.

Michael didn't care how much *that* cost him.

Even if it meant having those he loved most in

the world think he was a complete loser for another month or so. He was keeping quiet for all their sakes. The lawyers had been crystal clear about what happened to many lottery winners and why few, if any, people should know about the jackpot.

Even so, people were trying to figure out the winner's identity. A fired cashier from the winning convenience store had stolen a security camera video of people, including Michael, buying lottery tickets. The footage surfaced two days ago on the internet, but thankfully, he'd worn sunglasses and a beanie. Those things and the beard he'd grown since losing his job made him unrecognizable. But others from the footage had stepped forward to say they weren't the winner.

That was why his high-priced attorney from New York had told him to stay out of Charleston until the new year. That was when a representative of the trust planned to turn in the ticket and claim the prize money, but Michael had wanted to see his parents before he took off. He just hadn't expected an interrogation to be on tonight's dinner menu.

"It's going to be fine," he added.

"You keep saying that, but you have no place to live and no job." His mom wrung her hands. "We want you to know how much we love and accept you."

Mason nodded. "You're the best younger big brother ever."

That made no sense, but whatever. Michael smiled at him. "Thanks, bro."

"You always know when to show up with a pizza and a six-pack," Madison added.

His dad nodded. "You've been a binge drinker for a while now."

Huh? Michael stiffened. "I wouldn't say that. I don't party nearly as much as I used to."

His father's jaw tensed. "But you still do. Drink, that is."

Marley cleared her throat. "What Dad means is we're concerned you've been drinking too much and possibly doing more since you lost your job."

"Are you drinking and doing drugs?" his mom blurted.

Say what? Michael stared at each person who showed the same concern and... fear. His heart dropped.

Forget this being an interrogation.

This was an intervention.

How had this happened? Why was this happening? "No. Of course not."

"I saw your second cell phone on Sunday. Is that how you call your dealer?"

"I don't have a dealer." His temperature rose. Sweat beaded his hairline. He used the extra phone to contact his team, and it would become his permanent one after they collected the money, so he had better control of who had the number. This was all part of the attorney's plan, who had worked with big lottery winners for years. But his family didn't know that.

They couldn't know that.

Not yet.

As he dragged his hand through his hair, Michael considered what to say. This would be laughable, except they were so serious. "I appreciate the concern, but I promise I'm not doing drugs or drinking too much."

"That's what addicts say," Madison mumbled. "I've seen you drunk."

Rory kissed her forehead.

Seriously? They're really going to do this. Michael blew out a breath.

"And I've seen everyone in this room except Von drunk, including Mom and Dad, yet you don't see me accusing any of you of being…" He couldn't say it. "I drink a beer now and then. More on the weekends, but it's always been like that. I'm not a drunk or a druggie."

A vein throbbed on his dad's neck. "Your recent lifestyle suggests otherwise, especially sleeping somewhere different almost every other night."

"My friends aren't kicking me out." The words rushed out of Michael's mouth. He was compelled to defend himself, even if they were dead wrong. "I don't want to take advantage of anyone." And he planned to reward their generosity once he had his winnings.

"You could stay here," Mom offered.

He stifled a groan. "I'm too old to move back home. And there's no need for anyone to keep tabs on me."

Madison leaned forward. "Your eyes aren't bloodshot."

"Of course not. The last drink I had was here on Sunday night. It's none of your business, but I haven't taken so much as a pain reliever in months."

Once again, glances passed around the room.

This is unreal. "Do you want me to pee in a cup? Take a blood test? Because I get the feeling that's what you'll need to believe me."

"That's not funny, Mikey." His father's nostrils flared. "This is serious. We've checked into rehab centers and found space for you in one. We'll pay—"

"Unnecessary." He glanced at Von. "Please, help me out here. Your sister's boyfriend is an alcoholic, right?"

Von nodded. "Josh is sober and doing well."

"Happy to hear that, but it makes you the most experienced with this. Does anything in my behavior suggest I'm drunk or high or have a problem?" Michael asked him.

Von glanced at Marley, who nodded. "No, and

I mentioned that to everyone before you arrived."

Relief surged through Michael. At least someone was on his side.

"You show up on time. You haven't lost weight. You're dressing the same way you always have, other than the beard," Von continued. "And you don't smell like alcohol."

"Thank you." Except his future brother-in-law appeared to be the only one who believed Michael.

Part of him wanted to tell everyone the truth, but if word slipped out—accidentally at a holiday party or Christmas celebration—it would ruin all the plans his team was putting in place. If he collected the jackpot anonymously, people, including strangers, wouldn't ask for money. His family wouldn't be the target of scammers out to make a buck or steal from them. Monroe wouldn't need a bodyguard to keep some lunatic from taking him.

His mom's knee bounced. "If you're really okay and this is all a… misunderstanding, why won't you come with us to North Carolina for Christmas?"

Because I would have zero privacy and be unable to keep in touch with the people who are setting everything up for me. This was a critical time, and he wanted to be available if needed. Michael hated withholding the truth from her—from everyone. "There's stuff I need to do."

His mom's shoulders drooped. "What stuff is

so important it requires you to be alone for the holidays?"

This year was the first time the Patterson clan—including aunts, uncles, and cousins—wouldn't gather for Christmas in Charleston. Everyone was spending the holidays with their in-laws who'd been ignored for...

Well, forever.

His parents were spending the holidays with his mom's family in Asheville, while Mason and Monroe would travel with Ashleigh to Savannah. Madison was heading with Rory and his family to Colorado. Marley and Von were meeting his twin sister, Hope, and their parents in Berry Lake, Washington, to be with Josh Cooper and his family.

Michael preferred spending the next few weeks on his own, preparing for his new life. And though his team wouldn't be with him per se, they had web meetings and calls all the time. Which gave him an idea—one that might appease his mom. "Who said I'd be alone?"

Silence fell over the room. The only sound was the crackling wood in the fireplace.

Madison closed her gaping mouth. "Do you finally have a girlfriend?"

"I never said that."

"But your friends will be with their families over the holidays," Marley said.

"Who is she?" Ashleigh asked, her eyes full of curiosity.

"I bet she has blond hair and is a foot shorter than you," Madison said.

"Of course, she's petite and has blond hair," Ashleigh agreed.

Marley nodded. "Mikey has a definite type."

"But what about the second phone?" his mom asked.

Once again, his lottery win provided the answer—a truthful one. "I'm using it for business. That way I don't miss any calls, and I didn't have to make my voice mail greeting professional."

Mason nodded. "Yeah, those burps you have on there wouldn't go over well if someone wanted to set up an interview."

Suddenly, everyone talked over each other, laughing about their intervention and showing the same relief Michael felt. From addicted to attached in minutes. A good thing he loved them so much, but they *could* drive a person to drink.

The only problem?

There wasn't a girlfriend. Nor would there be one soon.

He didn't want to date or fall in love. Not with so many things changing in his life. And once he had the money, Michael had no idea how that might work. He didn't want to make someone he liked sign an NDA before they went out. Trust would be a big issue. Insurmountable, even.

But if his family wanted to believe he'd met a

woman, so be it—and in his defense, he worked with three women on his team. The dates on his calendar were for calls or meetings, not dinner or a movie, but no one needed to know that.

Finally, his family quieted.

"Do you want to stay at the house over Christmas?" The tight lines had disappeared from his mom's face.

Michael wished that were an option, but he had to get out of Charleston. "I'm thinking of driving to Myrtle Beach."

"That's too far. Why not spend the holidays in Indigo Bay?" Von asked. "You can stay at my house."

Marley straightened. "That's a great idea."

Von nodded. "We leave on the eighteenth for Berry Lake and we'll be back on the thirty-first in time to host the Pattersons' New Year's Eve party."

"You told me you love the place," Marley added as if Michael needed any convincing.

Von was a contractor. He'd remodeled the beachfront cottage in Indigo Bay after buying it from his parents, who were living in an RV and visiting every state.

A free place to stay less than an hour away? That should be far enough away from Charleston to give him anonymity. Michael smiled. "That would be great, but will Hope mind?"

"She's already in Washington, so the place will

be empty." Von flashed an encouraging smile. "When we spoke the other day, she mentioned something about finding a house sitter before the call dropped. It's fine. You can use my bedroom."

"This will be awesome." And cheaper than renting a place or booking a room somewhere, since Michael had a credit card, but cash was tight. He'd used his severance check to cover the initial retainer for his team. "Text me what you want done while you're away, and I'll take care of it, including getting things for the party."

Von grinned. "That would be great. I'll also need you to bring in the mail and water a few plants. I'll leave the Wi-Fi password on the kitchen counter. You can help yourself to whatever food is there. Not that there's much with Hope away."

"I can feed myself." Even if he ended up living off frozen pizzas and ramen since he wasn't much of a cook. "I appreciate it."

"I hung lights and garland on the front of the house and the rear deck, but we didn't put up a tree since we won't be there on the twenty-fifth."

As Marley side-eyed Von, she pointed to the tree in the corner. "Neither will my parents, yet they have one."

Von kissed her. "I can put one up before we leave."

"It's fine," Michael said. "I don't need a tree."

"Mikey." His mom's tone held a warning. "You love trees."

This wasn't worth fighting over. "I can get one myself."

"We have decorations in the garage," Von said. "I'll leave them by the door in case you want to use them."

Michael's gut instinct was to say no, but that wouldn't go over well with his mother. "Thanks."

"Yes, thank you so much." Relief shone in his mother's eyes. She fanned herself. "This evening has turned out better than I'd expected. And I'll worry less knowing Mikey is at your place than spending the holidays in a dive motel, shooting up somewhere."

Come January, he would remind his mom of what she just said.

"Me, too," he joked. "But the next time you plan an intervention, make sure you put out appetizers. I'm starving."

Everyone laughed.

"Seriously, I appreciate the love, but I'm doing great." And things would only get better—seven-hundred-million-dollars-minus-taxes better. "Please don't worry about me at all."

Come January, Mikey Patterson would shock each one of them.

In the best possible way.

3

On the evening of December eighteenth, Sheridan removed her suitcase from her mom's SUV. Bumper-to-bumper traffic filled the upper level at Portland International Airport. Between idling cars stopped in the right two lanes, people hugged goodbye—something she would do in a few minutes. She double-checked to make sure she had everything.

A horn honked.

She understood the impatience and the aggravation that accompanied the holidays. That was why she would soon be on a red-eye flight, heading from the Pacific Northwest to a state she'd never visited.

As her breath hung on the chilly air, Sheridan shivered. The thirty-degree temperature didn't cause the response, but a mix of anticipation and nerves. Even though she wanted to get away, knowing it was time to go made her insides twist.

She shut the hatch. "Thanks for driving me to the airport, Mom."

"Don't thank me. I enjoyed the time with you." The pompom on her mother's wool hat made her taller than Sheridan, who was five-ten in flats. "But I wish you'd change your mind about spending Christmas alone."

"This is what I want to do." She didn't hesitate to answer.

She didn't say "need" because her mom would only worry more. They'd discussed this for the past ten days, ever since she agreed to house-sit for Hope Ryan and her twin brother, Von, in South Carolina. Saying no never entered Sheridan's mind. She'd been desperate to get away from Berry Lake, which Hope seemed to sense. No doubt, the artist heard Deena's stories about Sal "firing" his daughter and "evicting" her from the apartment because of drug usage. The gossip had reached a ridiculous level, and Sheridan needed to escape the drama.

"A vacation will be good for me," she added.

Her mother sighed, a long, drawn-out exhale loud enough for people below in the arrivals area to hear. "This will be our first Christmas apart."

Since the divorce, Sheridan alternated

Christmas Eve and Christmas Day with her mom and dad, so each had her for one day. Most kids would have enjoyed opening presents and having stockings at both houses, but she would have preferred her parents together.

Not. Going. To. Happen. Now.

"Next year, I'm all yours." She forced a smile. "But you'll have Max's daughters with you this year."

No one knew how blending the families would work. Whereas Deena treated her as an enemy on sight, Max and his three daughters were the opposite. They tried as hard as Sheridan and her mom to make sure everyone got along. The Culpeppers were nice, especially Nell, who worked as an RN at the hospital and helped Sheridan move out of her apartment.

"They're sweet," her mom agreed. "But I'd enjoy having you home, too."

Except it wasn't Sheridan's home. Someone else bought that house years ago. Her mom had moved in with Max, and Sal did the same with Deena. Sheridan had been happy to have her comfy apartment, but that wasn't hers now.

Don't go there.

She raised her chin. "I'll text."

"Call so I can hear your voice." Her mom rubbed her gloved hands together. "I'll miss you so much."

"I'll miss you, too, but I'll be back on the thirty-first." Not that Sheridan had any idea what she'd return to other than her mom and stepfather's guest bedroom and a job or two that paid minimum wage. "I plan to figure a few things out while I'm in Indigo Bay."

"I'll pick you up and we can discuss it on our drive home." Her mom adjusted the collar on Sheridan's jacket. "Just remember, the new year is the perfect time to make a fresh start. You're talented, and any gallery would be lucky to have you as an employee."

Except there was only one in Berry Lake. She would have to leave her hometown to stay in the industry she loved, but how could she work for another place with no recommendation from Sal?

Not trusting her voice, Sheridan nodded. She wasn't sure if a fresh start would be enough given she had nothing left and needed a brand-new life. On the flip side, things could only go up from here.

At least she hoped so.

Her mom hugged her, wrapping Sheridan in warmth, softness, and the scent of puppies from the litter the rescue had taken in yesterday. Sheridan held on tight, not wanting the moment to end.

Her mom let go before she did, which was a first. "Do you have your driver's license and wallet?"

The question was so typical of Sabine

Culpepper. It didn't matter whether she was running the rescue or being a mom; she always checked to make sure nothing got missed. The woman was a combination of motherly love and warrior fierceness. Both kept the local rescue afloat when its survival had teetered for years.

Sheridan patted the leather backpack she was using as a purse during her trip. "In here. My credit card, too. Anything else I forgot, I can buy there."

"You'll be so far away."

The other side of the country, which was the point. "Hope said Indigo Bay is like Berry Lake. Quaint with holiday traditions, but it's located on the coast instead of near a lake and mountains."

"You know no one there."

Hope's twin brother, Von, would be on his flight west before Sheridan arrived in Charleston, rented a car, and drove to the beachfront cottage. She forced a smile.

"It'll be an adventure." And better than staying in a living nightmare, watching Remy steal her job, apartment, and father. A good thing Sheridan wasn't dating anyone, or her stepsister might have made a play for him, too. "I can't wait."

Her mother didn't appear convinced. "Whatever you do, be safe."

"I'll be fine." The words rushed out as much for Sheridan's sake as her mom's. "A quiet Christmas is what I need."

"I wanted both of your blended families to be a updated version of *The Brady Bunch*, but I realize how naïve I was."

Because of Deena, aka the evil stepmother, was implied but unspoken.

"We both were." Unfortunately.

But the sooner Sheridan put everything Sal did to her behind her, the better. She hadn't seen him since that Saturday in the gallery. In a town the size of Berry Lake, that took effort, but it reaffirmed that his new family meant more to him than she did.

Her breath hitched. She ignored it. "All we can do is move forward."

"Take those words to heart while you're away. Find your laughter. Sal stole that and your smile, along with everything else."

"I'll try." Sheridan had stopped crying two days ago, so that was progress. She'd needed the time to mourn. Part of her still hoped her dad reconsidered, but wallowing wouldn't solve anything. She didn't want to keep punishing herself for something out of her control.

Even if a part of her wished he would want her back at the gallery, at least.

Her mom's eyes gleamed. "You'd better get inside the terminal before you catch a chill."

"Thanks for everything you and Max have done and are doing for me." Sheridan's voice cracked.

Without them, she would be homeless. They'd also paid for her round-trip plane ticket from Portland to Charleston and rental car. "I love you."

"I love you, and I want you to have a merry Christmas." Her mom tapped the tip of Sheridan's nose. The gesture was one she used with her daughter and the animals who passed through the rescue. "Have faith, sweetheart. It may not feel like it now, but everything will work out the way it's supposed to."

Sheridan hoped so because her life couldn't get much worse.

Two flights, a layover, and not quite an hour's drive south, she arrived in Indigo Bay. The small coastal town was picture-postcard perfect with white lights and holiday decorations gracing the charming storefronts on Main Street. She recognized some of the names Hope had mentioned: Sweet Caroline's Café, The Chocolate Emporium, Happy Paws Pet Shop, Coastal Creations, Trixie Cone, and the High Tide Art Gallery. The town reminded her of Berry Lake with one big difference:

No snow.

That wasn't a bad thing since she had zero Christmas spirit. She hadn't told her mom, but Sheridan planned to call her on the twenty-fourth and then sleep and binge-watch her way through the twenty-fifth.

No tree. No gifts. Nothing to remind her of holidays past, and especially not the present one.

A good plan.

Now, all she had to do was pull it off.

A few minutes later, she parked her rental car—a white subcompact—in front of a charming beachfront cottage. Multicolor lights lined the eaves, and a wreath tied with a red ribbon hung on the front door. Pretty, but she would have preferred it if the place weren't decorated. No complaints, however; she was staying for free.

She yawned—something she'd done since the second flight when she hadn't fallen asleep again. A short nap wouldn't mess up her body clock too much, given the three-hour time difference. Even if she slept in tomorrow morning, all she *had* to do was deliver Hope's painting to a fundraising event. That shouldn't take long.

Sheridan exited the car. The temperature was in the high fifties. Much warmer than Berry Lake. A jacket would come in handy, but she wouldn't need the parka she'd carried on the plane. She rolled her suitcase to the porch, reached into her backpack, and removed the key Hope had given her.

Anticipation surged. Sheridan had finally arrived.

As she unlocked the front door, excitement replaced any lingering nerves. A turn of the knob and she stared at gleaming hardwood floors, overstuffed furniture, and gorgeous framed paintings hanging on the shiplap walls.

"Wow." She surveyed the open floor plan. "This is my kind of place."

Sheridan recognized the style of the paintings and the familiar name in the corners—Hope's. *Sal better follow through on the February exhibit he'd asked the artist to do.* Sheridan rolled her suitcase inside and closed the door.

The interior was more impressive now with the 360-degree view. Floor-to-ceiling windows along the far wall showed an overcast sky and the Atlantic Ocean. Hope mentioned the place was on the beach, but Sheridan hadn't expected it to be backyard close. Halfway to the glass, she let go of her suitcase and left it behind. The wheels might damage the floor.

As she stood at the window with a sense of awe, her breath left a patch of fog on the glass. Christmas lights and garland were strung along the deck. An unexpected sight with the beach grass, giving a touch of color to the sand below. Gentle waves rolled in. A couple with their dog walked along the beach.

"I'm not in Berry Lake anymore."

And that was A-okay. She would be—

Something crashed. A grunt followed.

The hair on the back of Sheridan's neck stood straight, and she whirled around.

A tall, bearded, shirtless man with wide shoulders and a broad chest rubbed his knee. He stared at her suitcase on the floor.

She gasped.

His gaze jerked to hers. Eyes widening, he straightened.

Icy fear flowed through her veins. Headlines about a murdered tourist in a charming beach house flashed through her mind. Her mom would blame herself for not stopping Sheridan from flying to South Carolina. Face it, nothing like this ever happened in Berry Lake. A break-in while people were on vacation or a broken car window when someone left valuables in plain view, but there hadn't been a murder in years.

Well, if she was going to die, she wanted to know who the killer was. She might be able to spell out the name in her blood before she lost consciousness. "Who are you?"

He didn't flinch. His eyebrows drew together. "Who are *you*?"

Sheridan searched for something to use as a weapon. A dining room chair was too heavy, and there was no centerpiece on the table. Her backpack hung off one shoulder. If she hit him with that, it might stun him long enough to escape, but her keys, ID, and phone were inside. All things she needed.

So, she balled her fist and raised her chin to add an inch to her height. He still towered over her, which meant he was six-two or three and muscled like an athlete. No way would she be able to take him, but she'd go down fighting.

Sheridan swallowed around the lump of fear lodged in her throat. "I asked first."

A beat passed and then another.

She held her ground.

"I'm Michael Patterson. My sister Marley is engaged to Von." His posture was ramrod straight. "Your turn."

Okay, this guy knew Hope's brother's name, so he might not be a psychopathic murderer.

Michael crossed his arms over his chest. "I'm waiting."

"Sheridan DeMarco. I'm house-sitting for Hope."

"Von asked me to house-sit."

That made no sense. "Hope gave me a key."

"Von gave one to me."

Stalemate.

That meant there was only one thing to do. It wasn't that early on the West Coast. "I'll call Hope."

His chest puffed out. "Go ahead but put it on speakerphone."

That had to be a good sign, right? Unless he wanted a witness to hear his killing spree without being able to identify him.

Sheridan removed her backpack from her shoulder, pulled out her phone, and unlocked the screen. A few seconds later, ringing sounded.

"Hey," Hope said. "Did you make it to the house?"

"I did, thanks, but there's someone else here."

"Von called me from the airport before he and Marley took off. He didn't mention anyone. Who's there with you?"

"It's me. Michael Patterson. Marley's younger brother," he said. "Von said you wanted him to find a house sitter, so he told me I could stay here while you were away."

"Ugh." Hope sighed. "I meant that I'd found someone to house-sit. Talk about miscommunication. I'm so sorry, Mikey."

Mikey? Sheridan glanced his way. The name didn't fit the guy at all.

"That's okay," he said. "Von mentioned the call getting cut off."

"Yes, I was out at the lake sketching," Hope explained.

"Service is bad there," Sheridan said.

"Lesson learned, but a little late for the two of you." Frustration filled Hope's voice. "What can I do to fix this?"

"Don't worry about it." The words flew out of Sheridan's mouth. Hope Ryan had wanted only to help. She didn't need to do anything from so far away. "We'll figure it out."

Michael side-eyed her. "But—"

"It's fine," Sheridan interrupted. "Don't give us another thought."

Michael frowned. His lower lip stuck out, making him look a lot more like a Mikey than she initially thought.

"Okay, but call if you need anything," Hope said cheerfully. "Merry Christmas!"

"You, too." That was all Sheridan could say. This year, Christmas might as well be a four-letter word. "Have fun with Josh and your family."

It was her turn to side-eye Michael.

"Merry Christmas, Hope." He was more cheerful than she expected. "See you on New Year's Eve."

"Looking forward to it." Hope sounded as if she was smiling. That was good. "Bye."

The line disconnected, and Sheridan lowered her phone. "We were both asked to house-sit."

"Yes," he agreed. "But I want to be alone for Christmas."

"So do I." Sheridan studied him. His flannel pajama bottoms hung low on his hips, showing off his V-shaped torso and flat, defined abs.

Hot.

His build had been threatening before she knew who he was. Now, she appreciated the eye candy standing in front of her. Except a guy who looked like him would never be alone for the holidays.

"Will your girlfriend join you here?" she asked.

"No. Just me. What about you?" He stared at her as if her skin mottled, and she grew gills. "Is your boyfriend joining you here?"

"It's just me." She glanced around the place. "So, how should we handle this?"

"One of us will have to leave." He crossed his arms over his chest.

If that was the guy's standing-his-ground pose, he needed to think again. "Not me. I just flew in from the West Coast. Hope is letting me stay here free for doing a few things for her."

"You can still do what she needs."

"I'm between jobs." Sheridan wasn't about to tell a stranger her life story, but she had to say something. "I can't afford to stay anywhere else."

His jaw jutted forward. "What if I paid for it?"

That wasn't what Sheridan had expected him to say. She would have enjoyed staying in this beach cottage with the to-die-for view of the Atlantic Ocean, but she didn't want to be around Michael. The feeling appeared mutual. "As long as the place is in Indigo Bay, so I can do what Hope needs me to do, that'll be fine."

4

"I'm sorry, we have no room at the inn."

Of course, they didn't. Michael almost laughed at the front desk clerk's words, except he still hadn't found Sheridan a room. She'd been napping for two hours, and he was no closer to finding her another place to stay than when he started.

He slumped on the breakfast barstool. "Thanks for checking."

"No problem," the woman said in a pleasant voice. "You might have a hard time booking a room at such short notice. A big fundraiser is happening this weekend, and Indigo Bay is a popular holiday destination. Everyone wants to make a wish on the community tree."

Oh, right. Von had mentioned the Christmas

Eve tradition. "Can I please get on your waiting list?"

"We don't have one, but you're free to check back as often as you'd like."

I figured, but maybe another place will come through. "Okay."

"I hope you find a room."

Me, too. "Goodbye."

He lowered his cell phone from his ear and reviewed the list of B&Bs, inns, motels, and hotels on Indigo Bay's website. He'd called each one with similar results.

No vacancies this weekend.

No rooms until the twenty-sixth.

Limited availability, but no consecutive nights.

Michael had no idea Indigo Bay was so popular at Christmastime.

His plan to have Sheridan a reservation when she woke up from her nap was a bust. Now, he might be the one to leave Indigo Bay, which sucked. This cottage was the best place for him to lie low for the next two weeks.

His phone rang.

Michael sat straighter. Had someone canceled a reservation?

He turned his screen up. The name belonged to his future brother-in-law.

Bummer, but Von might be able to connect Michael with a contact in town to find a room.

"Hey. Are you in Washington already?"

"Changing planes. Hope texted me about Sheridan being with you." Von sounded contrite. "Our twin connection failed big-time. Sorry for the mix-up."

"Yeah." Michael paused. He should follow Sheridan's lead and not blame Von or Hope. The twins needed to enjoy their holiday away, not worry about their house sitters. "But no big deal. It happens."

"Seeing her must have surprised you."

"Yep." Michael rubbed his knee where he'd bumped into her luggage. "I knocked over her suitcase and almost fell face-first on the floor."

"Ouch."

"My finely tuned balance helped me." The bruise would heal, but Sheridan might need time to get over her shock of his unexpected appearance. Her pale complexion and wide eyes had shown how afraid she'd been, but he respected how quickly she regained control. "But for a minute, I thought she would try to take me."

"She wouldn't stand a chance."

"Dude, I'd never hit a woman."

"Then it's a good thing she didn't try." Von laughed. "But I can't imagine a petite woman taking down the mighty Mikey Patterson."

An image of Sheridan flashed in his mind. "She's not petite. I'd say at least five-ten."

"Blond hair?"

Michael recalled the brown waves that fell past her shoulders. "Chestnut."

"So, not your type."

It was his turn to laugh. "Nope. I've never gone for the Amazon warrior woman."

Not that there was anything wrong with strong, tall women, but he wasn't looking for a girlfriend or even a date. He wasn't in the market for love, period. His life would change completely in a few short weeks. There would be plenty of time for a relationship and more later.

"Good, then your girl won't be jealous of Sheridan."

Girl? And then he remembered Tuesday night at his parents' house. Michael rubbed the back of his neck. He hated not being honest about dating someone, as everyone believed, but one thing was true. "That won't be a problem. But I'm not having any luck finding Sheridan another place to stay in Indigo Bay. Do you have any contacts?"

"Dallas Harper owns the Cottages. I've done some work for him."

"I called and spoke to Zoe Ward. They're full through New Year's Day."

"Sonja runs the Morrison Mansion B and B, but they're hosting a fundraiser this weekend."

"I called them, but they're booked." Michael wasn't too panicked, but the situation frustrated him. "All of the rental agencies are, too."

"It's going to be tough finding a place at the last minute with the holidays. Indigo Bay is popular at Christmastime."

"That's what everyone said, but Sheridan wants to be in town."

"You both should stay at the house. You're in my room. She's in Hope's."

Von made it sound so easy, but Michael gripped his phone. "We're strangers."

"You're friends of friends," Von countered. "Hope says Sheridan is the sweetest."

"Still strangers."

Von laughed. "True, but the place isn't that small. You won't be on top of each other, and there are two bathrooms."

But she seemed to want to be alone as much as Michael did. That left one other option—she stayed in Indigo Bay while he headed to Myrtle Beach. That had been his original plan.

"Do you have any questions about the list on the fridge?" Von asked.

Michael had found the Wi-Fi password, but he hadn't noticed a list. He went to the fridge and read the note attached to the freezer door with a hand-painted magnet. Most likely, one of Hope's that she made for a local shop.

"It makes sense." But the ten items required him to be in Indigo Bay, and some had to be done closer to the New Year's Eve party. He would need to stick around town. "I'll be finished by the thirty-first."

"Thanks, man." A boarding announcement sounded. "Before I hang up, Hope told me to tell you Sheridan has had a few rough weeks and is fragile, so be careful with her."

The adjective didn't fit the woman he'd met. She was the definition of solid. Sure, she'd mentioned being between jobs, but so was he. That was par for the course these days.

"Okay." Though Michael had no idea what being "careful" entailed. "She was falling asleep, so I told her to shower and nap while I called places."

Von whistled. "That will make Hope happy. She knows what it's like to have your life ripped away from you, so she wanted to help Sheridan."

Life ripped away? That sounded… worse than being unemployed. "Sheridan said she was doing something for Hope."

"Art things. An errand tomorrow and stuff in the studio. It'll give her something to do."

Michael got it. If Sheridan helped Hope, it would be easier for her to accept a free place to stay. Von was doing the same by asking Michael to help with the party prep. That made one thing clear. Marley was marrying into a kind family. Good, she deserved that.

"If Sheridan needs help with anything, I'll lend

a hand," Michael said.

"Great, Mikey. I knew I could count on you." Another announcement sounded in the background. "They just called our rows for the second time. Take care."

"Safe travels and merry Christmas." Michael disconnected from the call before slumping against the fridge. This house-sitting gig wasn't turning out as he'd expected. "Now what?"

"Is everything okay?" A quiet voice came from the living room.

He moved to the kitchen's entrance. Sheridan stood by the TV.

Michael wouldn't call her fragile, but she looked less like a fighter in her black leggings, oversized sweatshirt with a Van Gogh painting—he recognized it from a brand of vodka named after the artist—on the front, and fuzzy yellow-striped socks on her feet. She must not have dried her hair after the shower because strands stuck out. "Get enough rest?"

She yawned. "I could use more sleep, but I want to adjust to this time zone, so I set the alarm. Were you talking to someone?"

"Von. He called and apologized."

"That was nice of him."

"He's a great guy."

"Hope thinks the world of him."

"So does my sister Marley." Michael had always

49

felt bad for how their first relationship had ended between the now-reunited couple. It had been his sister's fault, and he was happy they'd worked things out.

Sheridan wiped her palms over her leggings. "So, I didn't unpack. I just need to put on a pair of shoes, comb my hair, and I'll be ready to leave. Well, as soon as you tell me where to go."

"About that."

Little lines formed between her eyebrows. "What?"

He might as well say it. "Remember that first Christmas, when Mary and Joseph had no place to stay? There aren't any rooms available in Indigo Bay."

Instead of laughing or even smiling, her complexion turned ghost white. Her bottom lip trembled; so did her chin. She jammed her hands underneath her arms, hugging herself.

"I don't know anyone in South Carolina except Hope, and she's not here." Her shaky voice matched the way she drew into herself as if trying to make herself smaller. "Where am I supposed to go now?"

Not fragile. Sheridan was afraid. She appeared ready to bolt, though he had no idea where she planned to go.

Michael hated to see her so frightened. Slowly, he moved closer until he'd cut the distance between them in half. "Hey, you're not going anywhere."

She eyed him warily. "I'm not?"

"You're not," he confirmed, hoping to lessen her fear. "You're staying right here."

Her mouth slanted. "Here, here?"

"In this beach house." He didn't want her second-guessing the situation.

Sheridan's expression didn't change. "You're not kicking me out?"

Her question explained her reaction and likely had to do with her life getting ripped apart. Whatever had happened to her, however, was none of Michael's business. He didn't want to make a new friend, but he wouldn't be a jerk about this.

"Of course not." Part of him was offended she'd think he would do that, but then again, she didn't know him. "This isn't my place. We were both asked to house-sit. That's no one's fault. Just a mix-up."

Sheridan licked her lips. "You want to be alone."

So did she, but he wouldn't bring that up with her so skittish. "Plans change. Von and Hope both need us to do things for them. I left my name on waiting lists, but they said it was unlikely any rooms would open up, so we'll have to share the house."

"Share it?" Sheridan spoke slowly as if testing out the words. "You and me? Here?"

That sounded like the last thing she wanted.

Michael, too, but that didn't stop him from nodding. "We'll stay out of each other's way."

She opened her mouth before closing it. She didn't appear happy about the situation. Well, neither was he, but what could they do?

"So, we just do our own thing while staying here?" she asked hesitantly.

Her uncertainty was unlike the woman who'd stood her ground when she first arrived earlier that morning. The difference was striking and worrisome.

"Yes, we don't have to talk, interact, or see each other that much." He hoped that put her at ease. "We'll have to share the kitchen and living room, but we can take turns or make some rules about the common areas."

Sheridan shifted her weight between her feet. She didn't appear convinced this would work. "I suppose we don't have another choice."

"There isn't if you want to stay in Indigo Bay and not live out of your rental car."

She sucked in a breath. "I don't want to do that. We can make rules now."

He'd been joking, but she appeared to take him seriously. Funny, since few people he knew did.

She lowered her arms. "We need paper and a pen."

"I'll get something from the kitchen." This wasn't how he thought the discussion would go, but he was the one who brought up rules. His family would die laughing at that. He held laughter back himself. But if having official ones written made her more comfortable, so be it. He grabbed the notepad and pen next to the landline, returned to the living room, and sat on the couch. "Take a seat."

She kept her arms crossed in front of her chest. "I'll stand."

He readied the pen. "So, what rules?"

"We don't go into each other's bedrooms or bathrooms."

With a smile, Michael wrote that down. "I have two older sisters, so I'm used to that one. Do you have any siblings?"

Sheridan angled her shoulders away from him. "We can each use a shelf in the fridge and take a spot on the counter for our food."

As he jotted down the next rule, he noticed she hadn't answered his question. "Works for me. I'm not much of a cook, so I bought easy stuff to make."

"I watch TV on my laptop, so I won't need to be in the living room."

"I prefer watching on the larger screen," he admitted. "Just tell me if you change your mind."

"I won't." The words shot out. "Are you planning to invite, um, company over?"

"Company?"

"Friends, a date." She swallowed. "A girlfriend."

"No to all three. And my family is out of town. What about you?"

"I don't know anyone."

"If you met someone?"

Her cheeks turned a charming shade of pink. "I wouldn't. I mean, I'm not here to meet... I just wanted to get away from my family and spend Christmas by myself."

The way her words rushed out one on top of the other was as cute as her blush. But what she said provided a few more clues about why she was in Indigo Bay. "No guests. Does that work?"

"Uh-huh." She stared at the floor. "And no walking around undressed."

It was a good thing he'd put on a shirt after she went to shower and nap. "And here I was planning to spend the next two weeks living in my underwear."

Her gaze jerked up to meet his.

"Joking." He tapped his pen against the notepad. "Anything else?"

"I'll do my best to stay out of your way."

"Me, too."

"Thank you so very much."

Her polite tone bristled because fear remained in her eyes. Michael didn't know her. He wasn't planning on getting to know her. But like one of the wounded animals or birds he brought home as a kid, he had to do something. "Look, neither of us expected to share a house with a stranger over Christmas, but all we can do is make the best of the situation."

"You mean being stuck together."

"Yes." He was glad she'd said it and not him, even if he'd thought it. He also remembered what Von had told him. Michael held up the list of their rules. "We'll each follow these, but if you need help with anything, just ask. I'm not from Indigo Bay, but I've been here a few times."

"Okay, thanks." She shifted her weight between her feet. "I'm going to the market to get groceries and then out to lunch."

"Sweet Caroline's Café has the best pies around," he offered.

Sheridan's expression softened. "That's what Hope said. Do you, um, want anything?"

He appreciated the offer, but their rules would make this situation easier to handle. Even if a slice of pie sounded delicious, it made little sense to run errands or do things for each other if they planned on keeping their distance. "I'm good, but thanks."

"Okay," she said. "I'll not see you later."

Michael laughed, surprised by her humor. That was something he might say. Sharing the beach house might work out better than he expected. "I'll not see you, too."

5

When Sheridan returned to the beach cottage, there was no sign of her new roommate anywhere. Relief flowed through her, bringing a much-needed smile. This trip was supposed to be about having alone time. She sure hoped they could stay out of each other's way.

As Sheridan carried two grocery bags to the kitchen, she relished the silence.

Crowds had filled both the café and store, and she waited ten minutes for a table and stood in the checkout line for at least that long at the market. That was surprising for a weekday in December. She'd dealt with customers and artists at the gallery so wasn't an introvert, but she'd hoped for a quiet vacation in Indigo Bay. Even though Hope had mentioned things to do, Sheridan expected the beach town would be near deserted. Now she found crowds and an unexpected roommate.

Was her Christmas meant to be blue no matter what she did? Well, it would if she planned on celebrating, which she didn't. She had no idea what Michael would do for the holidays, but she hoped nothing.

As she set the bags on the kitchen's breakfast bar, she noticed *Sheridan's food* scribbled on a sticky note. Michael must have done that, and he'd left her plenty of room to store her items. She hadn't been sure if he was humoring her about the rules, but this was nice of him. He might not be such a bro type as she initially thought.

In the refrigerator, she found an empty shelf with her name on it and placed her perishables there. She closed the door and then organized her food on the counter. If Michael continued to be so thoughtful, sharing the cottage wouldn't be so bad.

She arranged the lunch items—peanut butter, jelly, bread, and cookies. Those were her favorites growing up, and they were also easy on her wallet. She wanted to make sure she could afford a few meals out, even if she'd be eating by herself.

As Sheridan glanced at Michael's note, a ball of warmth settled at the center of her chest. He'd... surprised her. Everything about him reminded her of a frat boy. She hadn't been part of the Greek system at the University of Washington, where she received her art history degree, but she'd met a few fraternity brothers during her four years there. Though Michael was more attractive than any of those guys. She bet many artists would want to use clay or stone to bring his artistic build to life. Painters would enjoy capturing the way his features fit perfectly together. Handsome, yes, but she found cerebral, geeky guys with glasses and thinner builds more her style.

Not that she'd dated much since graduating college and returning to Berry Lake. Her focus had been on the gallery, so she put no effort into dating. Why should she when the results would be fleeting? Her parents' divorce had washed away any fantasies about finding her one true love and living happily ever after. Neither existed. Why even try?

She'd nearly laughed when Michael mentioned her meeting someone in Indigo Bay, because a date wasn't on her Christmas list. The only thing she wanted Santa Claus to bring her this year was a job that paid enough to afford an apartment of her own.

Sheridan grabbed a water bottle and opened the lid. The liquid was just what she needed.

"You're back."

The male voice startled her. She choked but somehow managed not to swallow the water

"Oops. I keep surprising you." Michael stood at the entrance to the kitchen. He wore black sweats full of holes and a stained, gray hoodie that had seen better days. Still, his easy grin would make most women take a second look.

Or swoon.

"It's okay." She wiped her mouth with the back of her hand. "I haven't had a roommate since my sophomore year of college, so I'm not used to having someone else around."

Well, not counting this month living with her mom and stepfather, but she didn't know if family technically counted as roommates.

He entered the kitchen, moving with more grace than he should have, given his size. "How did you like Sweet Caroline's?"

"Delicious. I'll go again."

His eyes lit up. "Be careful, or you'll become addicted. At least that's what Marley and Von tell me."

"Hope mentioned that, too, but what a way to go."

"Death by pie," he joked. "You'd have a smile on your face until the end."

Sheridan folded the two grocery sacks. He'd been polite with the rules, so she didn't want to leave a mess. "Thanks for saving a space for my stuff."

"No problem." He came closer, making the kitchen seem smaller. "Find what you need at the market?"

"I did." His soap and water scent tickled her nose. He must have showered, but his hair wasn't damp. She glanced at the food to stop herself from staring at him. "It's not as large as the one back home, but I found what I wanted."

"I stopped there yesterday and thought the same thing. You'll be eating well." He grabbed a blue box of macaroni and cheese from his stash. "Me? I go for quick and tasty. Especially for lunch."

"As long as you enjoy it."

"I do."

She watched him grab a pan from a lower cabinet. He appeared to know where everything was and wasted no movement. He had to be an athlete, but what sport?

Hands full, Michael motioned to the sink with his head. "Do you mind?"

"Oh." She was blocking his way. "Sorry. I'm going to unpack. Enjoy your lunch."

Ugh. And now she was rambling. She rushed out, went into her bedroom, and closed the door.

What is wrong with me?

Watching him captivated her. That made no sense.

Jet lag.

That would explain why.

A nap would help, but she needed to stay awake until bedtime to adjust to the new time zone faster. In the meantime, she would get settled in, take a stroll on the beach, eat dinner, and then sleep.

And most importantly, she would avoid Michael Patterson as much as possible. They'd set rules for a reason, and she didn't want to be the one to cause problems. If he asked her to leave, she had nowhere to go but home to Berry Lake. She wouldn't mess up this free place to stay in exchange for house-sitting and doing a few errands.

Which meant keeping her distance from her new roommate.

* * *

The next morning, a man's voice sent Sheridan bolting upright in bed and reaching for her phone to dial 911. Sunlight filtered through the half-open blinds, but she didn't recognize where she was.

Dazed and disoriented, she blinked.

Not her apartment. Wait, she hadn't lived there in three weeks.

This wasn't the guest room at her mom and Max's house, either.

Sheridan squinted, her gaze zeroing in on her suitcase. And then she remembered.

Indigo Bay.

Hope's cottage.

Michael.

Her temporary roommate.

He must be talking to someone.

As her muscles relaxed, and her panic lessened, she lowered the phone to the mattress.

She hadn't seen him when she made dinner and ate it at the breakfast bar. His door had been closed and he made no noise, so she assumed he was out. Though if he had been, she'd never heard him return.

A glance at her phone showed ten o'clock. Sheridan showered, dressed, and ate. Time to get her first job for Hope completed.

Each step Sheridan took toward the studio sent anticipation flowing through her. She loved everything about the art world—from the history to the proper way to display works—but she lacked the talent to create herself. The artist's process had intrigued her for years. So did their working space.

As she stepped inside, Sheridan shimmied her shoulders, feeling like a kid in a toy store, only a million times better. The faint scent of drying paint lingered on the air. It reminded her of touring a warehouse full of artist studios in Seattle. Each had been different, and she'd been mesmerized.

Even though Sheridan received detailed instructions about which painting to donate and the works to be cataloged, she took a moment to survey the area. Hope had mentioned how her brother, Von, had remodeled a spare bedroom to provide the perfect studio for her to work. Hope hadn't been kidding.

Tall windows and French doors to the back deck allowed natural light in. Paintings hung on one side, while others leaned against the same wall, and a few canvases sat on easels. The variety of sizes and subjects illustrated Hope's immense talent. To the right sat a built-in unit with shelves, cabinets, and a large counter. The utility sink was perfect for washing brushes and hands. Everything had been constructed with Hope's needs in mind and with love. The Ryan twins were fortunate to have each other.

Sheridan headed to the framed seascape of Indigo Bay, hanging on the far wall where Hope told her the oil painting would be. The view appeared to be from the back deck. The sun's position suggested morning. The picture captured the beach grass blowing in the breeze so realistically, she almost felt the wind against her skin. Two dogs ran across the sand near the waves rolling to shore.

Beautiful.

The piece should raise a lot of money for the animal rescue.

In the closet, she found the carton and materials she needed. A few minutes later, she carried the box outside, but unlike the SUV crossover she drove in Berry Lake, the four-door rental car's interior and trunk were both too small for the painting to fit.

What should I do?

Sheridan noticed Michael's much bigger SUV. It was older, in need of a wash, but big enough to fit the painting. Yes, they'd agreed to keep their distance, but this was—not an emergency—but a way to help a person who was helping her. If he said no, she would see which ride app was cheapest in Indigo Bay.

She returned inside and placed the box against the wall near the entryway. A glance down the hallway showed Michael's closed door, but music played. Not Christmas carols, but what sounded like classic rock. He must be awake because no one could sleep through that.

She knocked.

"Come in," he called out.

Sheridan did and froze.

He was in bed. A blue-plaid comforter covered part of his bare chest. Okay, this was his room, not common space, but this was the third time she'd seen him, and twice he'd been shirtless.

He yawned. "Hey."

His voice sounded sleepy, matching his bed hair that made him look even hotter.

What was wrong with her? She couldn't blame thinking of him this way on jet lag. "Sorry if I woke you. I heard the music, so I thought you were up."

"I've been hitting the snooze button for a while." He sat, sending the comforter onto his lap. "What's up?"

Oh, no. She stared at him as if she were seeing a man's bare chest for the first time. She'd seen this view yesterday, too. But she had to admit his broad, muscular shoulders appealed to her more than those of the men who hung out at Berry Lake's public beach.

Not helping.

She glanced around the room, trying to focus on anything except him. Her gaze landed on a Charleston RiverDogs bobblehead.

"Sheridan?" he asked.

"I need you." As soon as the words left her mouth, she cringed. She hadn't meant to say that. "Your help. I need your help. With Hope's painting. The box won't fit in my rental car. Your SUV looks big enough."

Ugh. She was rambling. Time to try again. "Would you mind driving me to the B and B this morning? It isn't far."

If only she'd started with that.

No biggie. In less than two weeks, she would never see him again.

"Do you want to go now?"

"Yes." The word shot out of her mouth. "I mean, sometime today. I'd like to get it dropped off sooner rather than later, but there's no rush."

As she pressed her lips together, she wondered about the odds of a hole opening and her falling inside. That might be a less painful way to go than facing Michael's scrutiny. Something about him disarmed her. That wasn't like her.

"Sure." He dragged his hand through his hair. "Let me take a quick shower first."

"Great. I'll wait in the living room, but don't rush." She hated bothering him and asking for his help, so she didn't want him to feel pressured. "We can go whenever you're ready."

Wicked laughter lit his eyes.

Her muscles bunched in anticipation of being teased or cut down. Deena and her minions had done that ever since the wedding. Sheridan had wanted to escape from that in Indigo Bay, but she would put up with anything Michael threw at her so she wouldn't disappoint Hope.

"I won't be long," he said. "I'll just need two sips of coffee before we leave."

Wait. That was… it?

She waited for the punchline—him saying negative stuff about her.

His forehead creased. "Is there something you want to say?"

"Thanks." As the word tumbled out of her mouth, the tension evaporated from her body.

"You're welcome."

Sheridan remained frozen in place, but she didn't know why.

"Anything else?" he asked.

"Enjoy your shower." No, that wasn't right. She would try again. "How do you like your coffee?"

6

As Michael drove Sheridan, he doubted a machete could cut through the thick tension in his SUV. The silence wasn't helping, but his radio hadn't worked in almost a year. He'd lost his aux cord, so he couldn't plug in his phone. A good thing the drive would only take a few minutes, or it would be more awkward.

He tightened his grip on the steering wheel, focusing on the road and not his passenger. He didn't need to glance at her to know she was studying her phone with a must-cram-for-finals intensity to avoid talking to him. Other than to tell him where they needed to deliver the painting to, she'd been doing the same thing since he walked into the living room.

Okay, I get it.

The way she'd acted in his bedroom embarrassed her. Her flushed cheeks and awkward mannerisms were signs of her attraction. She might not be his type, but he was flattered.

What man wouldn't be?

Maybe he should have worked harder to keep a poker face, but how she got all flustered and let the words flow was cute. Especially knowing he'd caused her reaction.

Her shutting it down disappointed him. But relief quickly followed because having his temporary roommate hit on him would complicate their house-sitting situation fast.

Sure, she was pretty. And face it, her faded jeans showed off her curves hidden by her sweatshirt yesterday.

If it were another time, he might want to get to know her. But he didn't need any new friends. Nor did a holiday romance fit into his plans.

"*Your destination is one hundred feet ahead on your right*," the robotic voice of her phone stated.

Not that he needed the directions, given the size of Indigo Bay, but at least someone didn't mind talking to him.

Michael parked across the street from the B&B. The driveway and curb spots in front were full of vans and trucks. He set the parking brake and pulled the key from the ignition. "Do you know where to drop off the painting?"

"The ballroom. I'm supposed to find Sonja."

Sheridan didn't raise her gaze from her phone, but at least she'd answered him.

"Thanks for the ride," she continued. "I need to set up everything, so there's no reason for you to stay. I'll walk back to the house."

She finally glanced his way. Her eyes were wide and her jaw tight.

He fought the urge to wrap his arms around her and squeeze tightly. His sisters appreciated his bear hugs when something bothered them. But Sheridan wasn't family or even a friend, and she was nothing like Madison or Marley. That meant touching her would be inappropriate. Besides, he didn't want to put her more on edge, but there was one thing that might make her feel better.

"I'll carry the painting inside." Sheridan was wound so tight, she might spring up like a jack-in-the-box. His helping would protect her and Hope's donation. Besides, he had nothing else to do today. His team didn't work on the weekends, and a guy could only play so many video games or binge-watch TV series. "My day is wide open. No plans or places to be."

Without waiting for a reply, Michael got out of the car. He didn't need his beanie in the fifty-degree temperature, so he wore a baseball cap instead. He'd ditched his sunglasses because he hadn't wanted to draw attention to himself. The beard hid his face, anyway.

He met Sheridan at the back of the SUV, where he removed the box before closing the hatch. "Lead the way."

She hunched. "I have no idea where I'm going."

"Follow your gut."

Her gaze narrowed. "Is that what you do?"

The fateful trip into the convenience store to spend money on a snack he hadn't needed came to mind. But his gut had told him to buy a ticket, too. "Yeah, it is."

"I've always been more... methodical. But things haven't worked out like I'd planned. I might try your way."

"You should." He waited for her to move. She didn't. "So, what's your gut telling you?"

"The front door would be a good place to start."

He grinned. "See?"

"I'm sure it's more common sense saying that." Still, she continued toward the B&B's entrance. Candy cane lights lined each side of the walkway. "This is beautiful."

"It is." White bulbs lined the eaves of the old house that had found new life thanks to a meticulous renovation. A large wreath hung on the front door, scenting the sea air with the smell of sharp, fresh pine, and provided an elegant touch of holiday cheer. "My sister Marley is an architect. She told me the place was once on the town's condemned list. The new owners remodeled it, and the B and B opened in July."

"They did a fantastic job." Sheridan glanced over her shoulder at him. "Have you been inside?"

"No. When I'm in Indigo Bay, I sleep on Von's couch or floor. Since he's away, I upgraded to his bed." Not that Michael minded where he slept. That might change, but he didn't think by much. He was the definition of casual. He owned one suit—a present from his parents his senior year of college for weddings and job interviews. He much preferred comfort over style for both his clothes and vacations. "I'm more the stay-in-the-cheapest-room-since-we'll-never-be-in-there type, so I'll have more money to spend."

"Makes sense, especially if you're only sleeping and showering someplace."

She hadn't struck him as a roughing-it traveler. "What about you?"

"I haven't traveled lately. My mom doesn't go out of town because of the animal rescue, though Max, her new husband, is trying to talk her into a delayed honeymoon." Sheridan got a faraway, almost sad look in her eyes. "My dad used to take me to galleries and museums all over the world. He would find out-of-the-way unique places to stay at. I never considered the cost because he paid."

"A perk of traveling with parents."

"It was." Her voice cracked.

What Von mentioned yesterday popped into Michael's mind. Something might have happened to her father.

Sheridan rang the bell before he could ask.

The door opened. A woman around fifty with tousled, dark-blond hair smiled. "Welcome to the Morrison Mansion B and B."

"Hi. I'm Sheridan DeMarco." Her voice was strong, and she stood tall, not hunching her shoulders or trying to hide as before. "I'm looking for Sonja. I have a donation from Hope Ryan."

"I'm Sonja." The woman was dressed impeccably with perfect makeup. She appeared more ready to attend an event than host one. "Hope mentioned someone would be by. I have a display easel set up, though I know art folks are particular about lighting and positioning."

Sheridan laughed.

The sound was unexpected, and it was something Michael wouldn't mind hearing again.

"Did Hope warn you about that?" Sheridan asked.

Sonja motioned them inside. "No, but I've had a few art connoisseurs as guests. I thought one couple would ask me to rehang the artwork before they checked out."

Michael followed Sheridan inside. The scent of pine with hints of cinnamon and vanilla lingered in the air.

"Sounds like there's more to it than making sure the top isn't crooked," he joked, knowing his framed prints and posters were never straight, and it didn't bother him at all.

"According to those guests, there is," Sonja said.

Sheridan moved toward the staircase where a lighted garland decorated an oak banister. "Your B and B is lovely."

Sonja's smile widened. "Several hands were involved in the renovations, and I'm thrilled how everything turned out."

"Great Christmas decorations," Michael added, suddenly missing having a tree at Von's house.

"Thank you," Sonja said. "This is our first holiday with guests. We wanted the holiday décor to add to the atmosphere but not overwhelm it."

Sheridan reached toward a holly leaf on the garland before placing her arm at her side. "It works."

"Follow me." Sonja led them into the ballroom.

Michael followed the women into the large space. Christmas music played. He'd been in hotel ballrooms, but this was like he'd stepped into a holiday movie that his mom and sisters enjoyed watching. Yes, they'd made him watch, too, and they didn't suck.

"Wow." He glanced around. People placed silver and red centerpieces on the forest-green linen-covered tables. The Christmas tree with white lights needed to be decorated. There was even a stage. The only thing missing was snow and the guy in red with a hearty *ho-ho-ho*. "This is swankier than I thought it would be and totally Christmassy."

Sonja beamed. "We were fortunate to have sponsors for tonight's gala. Which is great since the rescue desperately needs to expand their building. All funds raised will go to that."

"That's impressive." Sheridan's tone matched the awe of her expression. "My mom runs a rescue, but her events aren't anything like this."

"Ours normally aren't, but we figured we'd try it." Sonja pointed to a Barks and Bows sign. "There's also an adoption and holiday fair on Tuesday if you're curious how the rescue runs a lower-key event."

"Thanks for telling me about that." Sheridan surveyed the ballroom as if memorizing the details. "My mom's always looking for new fundraising ideas. I'll check that out and take notes for her."

"Oh, you should do that. It will be fun. People are welcome to bring their pets and have photos taken with Santa. There will also be booths selling gifts and holiday items." Sonja headed to the opposite side of the ballroom where rectangular tables were pushed together to make a long row. An empty display easel stood at one end. "This is where the silent auction is being held. You can set up the painting on the easel. Leave the box under the closest table, and we'll package the painting for the winner."

Michael took that as his cue. He placed the box on the hardwood floor and then stepped back to give Sheridan space.

"Do you need anything?" Sonja asked.

"No, thanks." Sheridan kneeled, not wasting a minute. "I'm sure you have a hundred things to do before tonight, so we'll see ourselves out."

"I do, so I appreciate that." Sonja looked at Sheridan and then Michael. "It's nice meeting you."

"Same," Michael said. "Have fun tonight."

Sheridan opened the box. "I hope the rescue reaches its fundraising goals."

Sonja gave a slight wave of her hand. "I hope I see you on Tuesday."

As the woman walked away, Sheridan removed the painting. "Would you please check that the display is steady?"

"Sure." Michael gave the display a shake and pressed down on the shelf where the painting would rest. Each of the legs looked secure, too. "It's solid."

"Thank you." She uncovered the painting and carefully placed it on the silver easel. "Black wouldn't stand out as much against the frame, but this should work."

"It looks great." He studied the painting,

noticing details that made him peer closer. "I've seen some of Hope's works, but I like this one. Von told me he wants her to do shows again."

"She has such a distinctive style that appeals to a variety of people. She'll get the recognition she deserves. It won't be long until she'll be turning down galleries who want to exhibit her work."

"You sound confident." Michael enjoyed seeing this side of her. It contrasted nicely with her adorable blushes and rambles from before.

"I am." Sheridan didn't hesitate to reply. She stepped back and then shook her head. "I need to position the display, so the lighting enhances the canvas rather than distracts from it."

He laughed. "Sonja was right."

"Yes, but this is my job."

Wait. He thought she was unemployed. "You're an artist?"

"Only in my dreams." Sheridan half laughed before adjusting the easel a few inches. "I work in a gallery. Well, I used to work in one."

No wonder she'd sounded so confident. Sheridan had the experience to back up what she said about Hope.

She stepped away again. Two lines formed over the bridge of her nose. "Still not right."

It looked good to Michael, but the "dogs playing poker" print was his idea of fine art. "Need help?"

"I've got it." Sheridan moved the display one way and then another. Her forehead creased with each adjustment. As her tongue stuck out between her teeth, she scooted everything an inch if he was generous. She stared at the painting for what felt like ten minutes. In reality, it was seconds before she took a photo with her cell phone. "All done."

"Are you sure?" he teased because the setup looked perfect to him. "It might be off by an eighth."

Sheridan laughed, and once again, the sound wrapped around him.

"Sorry, not sorry." Her eyes twinkled. "This is nothing compared to the care that goes into preparing for an exhibit. Sometimes an artist wants a say, but it's often just me knowing people will scrutinize everything, so I don't want to make a mistake. But it's essential to show off a painting in the best light, literally. That doesn't sway some art lovers. They love a work and want it. But others are more technical in their decisions. It can make or break a sale."

"Which are you?"

"I can't afford an original painting like this one, but if I fell in love with a work, I doubt anything else would matter." She stared longingly at the painting. "But working with paintings and artists is the next best thing. Or it will be when I find another job."

"Does your town have more than one gallery?"

"No." As the word shot out, her cheeks turned a charming pink. She placed the box and the padding underneath the nearest table. "My dad's is the only one in Berry Lake."

Her dad's... The pieces clicked together in Michael's mind. "You used to work for your father?"

She nodded. "He was going to fire me last month, but I quit so I wouldn't be forced to train my stepsister, who he hired to take my place."

Michael whistled. "And I thought I had family issues."

Her gaze snapped to his. "Did you work for your dad?"

"No. My family is just..." He didn't want to bring up the intervention because that would only raise more questions. "Nosey. They're also upset I haven't found a job after the company I worked for closed a couple of months ago."

"At least they care about you."

Michael thought about her words. "You're right. They do."

"You're lucky. My dad is only interested in his new wife and her children, who are adults. I no longer matter."

"That sucks."

"It does, but I had fewer Christmas gifts to buy this year because of that." Sheridan kept her tone light, but her gaze darkened.

He kept his arms at his sides, or else he would have touched her. "I'm sorry."

"It happens." She brushed her palms together. "I'm finished. We can get out of here now."

Sheridan made a beeline to the exit without a glance his way.

He quickened his pace to catch up with her. "I hope I didn't upset you."

"You didn't." She kept moving toward his car. "It's just... hard."

Michael wasn't sure what to say. "Do you want to talk about it?"

She shrugged. "I always thought the evil stepmother was an urban legend or a plot device in cartoons. But thanks to mine, I went from having my dream job to filling in whenever the local cupcake shop is short on staff, volunteering at the rescue, babysitting, doing whatever else will pay a few dollars, and..."

"House-sitting."

She nodded. "My dad gave my apartment to my stepsister, so I moved in with my mom and her new husband."

"No wonder you wanted the beach cottage to yourself." They passed a delivery person carrying boxes. "I've been couch-surfing, but my friends are at work during the day."

Sheridan smiled. "We're a pair."

"We have a lot in common." Which surprised him.

"Unemployed and homeless."

That made him laugh. He had a feeling the situation bothered her more than it did him. "Are your brothers and sisters giving you a hard time?"

Her mouth slanted. "I'm an only child, though now I have seven new stepsiblings between my parents' two blended families."

Oh, man. That would take some getting used to after being the only kid her entire life. "I can't imagine what that must be like. I've always had my brother and sisters."

She laughed. "Are you the oldest?"

"The youngest, but they call me their 'big' brother because I'm taller than any of them."

Sheridan stopped to straighten one of the candy cane lights. "That's cute."

He shifted his weight between his feet. "I guess, but as a kid, I was self-conscious of being bigger than everyone else."

"They also call you Mikey?"

He cringed. "Yes. It was fine when I was seven, but I fear that nickname will never go away."

"Ingrained in your family?"

Michael nodded. "DNA level."

She crossed the street. "You seem more like a Michael than a Mikey to me."

"Thanks, some of my friends call me Mike. Dude or bro works."

Sheridan laughed. "Were you in a fraternity?"

"Yep, were you part of Greek life?"

"No."

"That's a firm no."

"Not my thing."

His SUV was about twenty feet away from them. He removed the key fob from his pocket. "Do you need to go anywhere else?"

Her gaze went from his car to him. "I think I'll walk to Sweet Caroline's."

"You're addicted."

"I didn't say what I was ordering."

"Okay, I made a huge assumption," he relented. "But am I wrong?"

A beat passed. "I don't know yet."

"That means you want pie." Michael hadn't had breakfast, and he was hungry. "Pie this early might be a little much, but a cinnamon roll sounds good. Want some company?"

7

Ten minutes later, Sheridan stood in line with Michael at Sweet Caroline's Café. The scent of brewed coffee and fresh-out-of-the-oven baked goods filled the air. Her nose enjoyed the tantalizing smells, but her stomach was impatient for a snack. She glanced at the people behind her. "It's more crowded today."

"It always is on the weekends, but the line is out the door during holidays and the summer."

She moved forward two steps. "Hope never mentioned that."

"This is her hometown. She's used to the crowds, and she works from home, so it probably doesn't bother her. Lines annoy Von, but he still loves the place, so he puts up with them. At least, according to Marley."

One good thing about so many customers was the conversations nearly drowned out the holiday music playing. Sheridan hadn't been able to ignore the decorations at the B&B, but here, she could almost pretend Christmas wasn't on its way. "You're close to your family."

He nodded. "We have dinner at my parents' house every Sunday. I usually see one of my sisters during the week, too."

Until moving in with her mom, they rarely saw each other unless Sheridan was volunteering at the rescue, but they texted or spoke each day. "Do you live near each other?"

"In Charleston. Though after Marley and Von get married this coming summer, she'll move here."

"What about Hope?"

"Von thinks Josh will propose soon, and Hope will move to Berry Lake."

"The Coopers are a tight-knit family."

"Von mentioned that's why they're in Washington for Christmas."

"Lucky for you and me."

Michael's blue-eyed gaze met Sheridan's. "Very."

Her heart bumped, and everything around her faded until it seemed to be only the two of them standing there. *You* and *me* suddenly felt more like *us*. She swallowed.

"Keep the line moving, guys," someone said behind them.

The voice startled Sheridan. She blinked, breaking the connection between them.

Uh-oh. They weren't alone, yet for a minute, she'd been transported... somewhere else.

"It's not like by moving we'll reach the counter any faster," Michael whispered to her.

As his warm breath brushed her neck, tingles formed in her stomach.

She gulped. What was happening?

"Have you spent much time in Charleston?" he asked, seemingly unaffected by the shared moment.

Sheridan coughed to clear her dry throat. "Long enough to grab my luggage and get a rental car."

"You should spend a day there." He acted more like a fraternity guy rather than a man who'd mesmerized her and appeared as captivated by her as she'd been of him. "It's a short drive from Indigo Bay."

Less than an hour if the touristy spots were near the airport. "Maybe I will."

Though sightseeing with someone would be more fun. Someone who knew where to go. Someone like... him.

Dare I ask?

No, that would be weird with them staying out of each other's way. Still, a part of her waited to see if Michael offered to show her around. He said nothing. Instead, he focused on the menu board hanging on the wall behind the counter.

So much for hoping.

She shouldn't be surprised. They weren't on a date. They also weren't friends. They were two strangers sharing a beach cottage.

Her shoulders slumped until she straightened.

There was no reason for her to be disappointed.

Whatever *moment* she'd imagined between them must have been one-sided. She was hungry. Hunger would explain her reaction to him. It was a good thing they were almost to the front of the line, so she could eat.

"I'll write down where you should go," he offered.

"That would be better than a list off the internet."

"Much better. I'll schedule a reminder." He typed on his screen and then stuck his phone in his pocket. "I've lived in Charleston my whole life. It's a great city."

Something in his tone sounded off. "Do I hear a 'but' coming?"

"That obvious, huh?" Michael adjusted the brim of his cap. "But, I'm not ready to put down roots just yet."

A family of five stepped away from the counter, so she moved forward again.

"Is there somewhere else you want to live?" she asked.

"No, but I want to travel." His eyes brightened.

"See the world."

"That would be fun."

He nodded. "My family lives in Charleston, but that might not be the right place for me. I need to figure that out."

A sigh welled inside her, but she didn't allow it to escape. "I wish I had your sense of adventure."

His gaze narrowed. "You're not working right now. What's holding you back?"

It was a good question; she had no job or a place to call home. Yet...

"I've lived in Berry Lake my entire life except for the four years I was away at college." She pictured her mom. Some friends had never left. Others had returned to town. "Almost everyone I know is there. I can't imagine living anywhere else, but if I want to work in a gallery, I won't have a choice."

"That's a rough spot to be in."

"I hate it." Which was why a slice of pie sounded better with each passing second. "I don't want to have to live with my mom and her new husband, so I need to decide what I should do while I'm here."

"You just arrived. Don't put pressure on yourself."

Easier said than done. "I know, but a part of me—"

She pressed her lips together.

"What?" he asked.

Oh, boy. She hadn't meant to say that. "Part of me hopes my father changes his mind, and things go back to the way they were."

"Will he?"

"No." That was the truth, especially with Remy living in the apartment and working full-time at the gallery. "It's been three weeks. No rumors suggest things aren't working out. So, if I listen to my gut, the answer is no."

Michael's expression softened. "Does your heart agree? That's what my sisters would ask."

A lump formed in her throat. She swallowed around it. "Honestly? I have no idea. I'd like to believe he would come to his senses. I mean, fathers are supposed to love their kids, right?"

Michael placed his hand on her shoulder. "They are."

His touch comforted her. It was all she could do not to lean in to him. But she needed to handle this situation on her own. Her mom had Max now. They might be in their fifties, but they were also newlyweds. Sheridan didn't want to be a burden. She straightened.

"I'll figure it out." She would keep telling herself that until she had. "So, are you going to travel now or later?"

"In the new year." A wide grin spread, lighting up his face and taking her breath away. "With no job to tie me down, I have the freedom to do whatever I want."

"You're fortunate." He must have received a generous severance package. Sal hadn't paid her for the days she'd worked that last week, saying it was in lieu of a two-week notice.

People heading to the door walked by on their left. She moved out of their way.

A woman smiled at her. "Merry Christmas."

Ugh. Sheridan forced the corners of her mouth upward. "Same to you."

Okay, repeating the words wouldn't kill her, but she wasn't in the holiday mood.

The two men in front of them stepped up to the counter to order.

"Where would you go if you had the chance and money was no object?" Michael asked.

"Where *wouldn't* I want to go?" Chills formed on Sheridan's arms thinking about having the ability to travel with no concerns about affording it. "There are museums all over the world. I'd build an itinerary around all the art I've dreamed of seeing in person."

"You love art."

"It's my passion." And she'd better stop before she rambled again. "Where do you want to go?"

He rubbed his fingers over his beard. "I might let my taste buds decide."

She wouldn't have guessed that based on what

he ate yesterday. "A foodie, huh?"

"Nah." He winked. "I just like to eat."

The men ahead of them stepped aside.

"Hello, welcome to Sweet Caroline's Café." A fifty-something woman greeted them with a smile. Her gaze zeroed in on Sheridan. "I've seen you in here before. You're new in town or visiting?"

"Visiting. I'm from the Pacific Northwest."

"Lovely part of the country. Very wet and green." Caroline exuded small-town warmth. "What brings you to our little spot of heaven in South Carolina?"

"I'm house-sitting."

"For?" Caroline asked, which brought a chuckle from Michael.

Sheridan guessed people enjoyed knowing everyone's business as they did back home. "Hope Ryan."

As Caroline's forehead creased, she looked at Michael. "You're Marley's brother."

It wasn't a question. "Yes, ma'am."

Caroline focused on Sheridan again. "Von told me Mikey was house-sitting for him."

Michael's posture went ramrod straight. The woman's use of his nickname must have caused the reaction.

"He is, too," Sheridan clarified. "There was a miscommunication with Hope."

Caroline's gaze bounced between her and him.

"So, you both…"

"Are house-sitting together," Michael said.

The woman clapped her hands. "Neither of you will be alone for the holidays. How wonderful!"

That was one way to look at it. Sheridan nodded.

Caroline's fingers hovered over the cash register. "Before I tell you the must-dos in town, let me take your order."

Michael motioned for Sheridan to go first.

She studied the menu. The cinnamon roll sounded delicious, but so did pie. "I'll have a slice of peach pie and a coffee."

"For here or to go?"

She looked at Michael. "Here?"

He nodded.

"What do you want, Mikey?" Caroline asked.

"We're not together," he said in a matter-of-fact tone.

His words stung more than Sheridan cared to admit. "Order what you want. I'll pay since you drove me to the B and B."

He hesitated. "Thanks. I'll have a cinnamon roll and a coffee."

Caroline passed the order to a young red-haired barista, took Sheridan's twenty-dollar bill, and rang up the total. "Now, the first thing you must do is buy an ornament for the community tree. On December twenty-fourth, people line up to make a wish on their ornament and hang it. Then, at five o'clock, our wonderful mayor will turn on the Christmas tree lights."

"Hope mentioned the ornaments."

"The wishes are the biggest part of the tradition and why folks return each year." Caroline handed over the change before leaning over the counter and lowering her voice to say, "Christmas wishes are stronger than birthday ones."

Michael snorted.

Sheridan elbowed him. "I hadn't heard that."

"Marley never mentioned it," he chimed in.

"Well, she might not have known that since she dumped Von, so they were apart last Christmas." Caroline shrugged. "At least they're back together and getting married this summer."

Not knowing what to say, Sheridan nodded.

That seemed enough for Caroline, who motioned to the area with tables. "Take a seat. Someone will bring out your food."

They found an empty table and sat.

Michael laughed. "Marley told me some people hated her for breaking Von's heart, but I assumed she was kidding."

"Caroline must be fond of Von. She seems the motherly type."

He nodded. "And Marley did a number on him, so I understand. He's a good guy."

"He sounds like it, to travel across the country

to have Christmas somewhere else."

"Von and Hope are tight. It's a twin thing."

"How does your family feel about being apart?"

"This is the first year the Patterson clan isn't celebrating Christmas together. Usually, we have extended family gatherings from Christmas Eve until New Year's Eve, but everyone decided to visit their in-laws instead."

"I guess we're meant to be here."

Another barista, a teenager with his hair pulled back in a man bun, placed their coffee cups and food on the table. "If you need anything else, please let us know."

Sheridan's mouth watered. The pie was just what she needed.

"I knew you would order that."

"I'm going to savor each bite." She scooped up a forkful and then stopped, holding it in mid-air. "You don't have in-laws, so why are you in Indigo Bay and not with your parents?"

"This is the perfect time for me to make plans for the new year." He added a pat of butter to his cinnamon roll. "I also didn't want to be surrounded by my mom's family in North Carolina. It would be too crowded and noisy."

Sheridan swallowed her pie. "It's funny. We're living parallel lives."

"It must be fate." He raised his mug in the air. "Here's to being homeless, jobless, and clueless about what comes next."

She tapped her coffee against his. "You make that sound almost fun and not so overwhelming."

"Hey, we're staying in a great beach cottage, in a quaint town, and it's Christmastime. What's not fun?"

"The holidays part."

Wide-eyed, he set his cup on the table. "You don't like Christmas?"

"I wouldn't say that." She ate another bite of pie.

His food remained untouched. "What would you say, then?"

"I don't like it this year."

He shook his head. "Nope."

"Excuse me?"

"You're not skipping Christmas."

She didn't understand how he knew that was what she wanted to do. Not that it mattered. "I am."

"No." He leaned forward. "Your father took your job and your apartment. Don't let him take Christmas from you, too."

As her jaw dropped, Michael's words swirled in her head. Talk about a lightbulb moment. "I never thought about it that way, but you're right."

"I usually am." With a satisfied grin, he ate a bite of his cinnamon roll.

Sal had taken so much from Sheridan. Did she

want to give him Christmas, too? "Not that it matters now, since I'm on the opposite side of the country from my mom."

"Hey, what about me?"

"You?"

"We can celebrate Christmas together."

She stiffened. "We're staying out of each other's way."

He grinned. "We did last night, but that hasn't worked so well today."

"True." That didn't mean he wasn't offering out of pity for her. Her insides twisted. "But we don't have to change anything."

"No, except I'm enjoying getting to know you." He sounded sincere. "It would be fun to spend more time together."

Fun. That appeared to be one of his favorite words. She used to enjoy having fun. Maybe she was allowing Sal to take even more from her. Still, she hesitated. "Yesterday, you were adamant about wanting to be alone."

"Today, I'm changing my mind." He set his fork on the plate. "We don't have to make a big deal out of Christmas. We're both unemployed, so no presents, but we can go to the ornament-hanging thing on the twenty-fourth and get a tree for the house. Von left out ornaments for me. What do you say?"

Anticipation made her shift in her chair. For the

first time in weeks, the dark cloud over her parted, giving her a glimpse of clear skies. "That does sound fun."

"We can see what stuff Von has and get a tree tomorrow."

She took a closer look at the decorations in the coffee shop. Even a few items made a big difference. "Caroline probably knows where to buy a tree."

"We'll ask her on our way out."

A contentment Sheridan hadn't experienced in weeks settled over her. Embracing Christmas instead of ignoring it might be what she needed right now. And she had one person to thank—Michael. She'd never believed in fate, but maybe she and Michael were meant to share the cottage together.

8

On Sunday afternoon, Michael inhaled the scents of sap and pine. It reminded him of when he hiked with friends a month ago, but he wasn't in a forest today. He stood in a corner lot with Sheridan, who beamed brighter than a gold star tree topper, reaffirming his suggestion to celebrate the holiday together was the right one.

So what if he couldn't remember the last time he'd gone shopping for a tree? It was probably when he was in high school; his parents took care of that, but not much had changed since then.

Christmas carols played. Two women wearing candy cane–striped aprons, Santa hats, and snowman name tags, stood behind a table covered in tree needles underneath a white pop-up tent, decorated with garland and lights. The table held bottles of tree food, packages of mistletoe, a cash box, and cups of coffee.

As people made their way up and down the rows of trees, a kid skipped while another spun with her arms extended. Two men debated the merits of a tree. One thing, however, was the same—everyone was smiling.

As Sheridan studied the price board, she shook her head. "We're definitely not in Berry Lake."

"More expensive than home?"

She nodded. "But since we're splitting the cost, it won't be that big a hit. And a few trees are on sale. We should buy one of those."

Her tone was upbeat, but a weight pressed against him.

Just pay for the tree.

That way, she wouldn't worry about money, and she could buy the tree she wanted. So what if his winnings wouldn't hit his account for a few weeks? His team hadn't decided what date a representative from Michael's trust would turn in the ticket, but they would soon, according to his most recent phone call with them.

"We don't have to find one on sale." He didn't have a lot in his bank account, but he had a credit card and planned to pay off the growing balance once he claimed his winnings. "I'll get the tree."

Her hands flew to her hips. "You'll do no such thing. We're in similar positions, and we agreed to split it."

They had, but that was before she'd mentioned the price.

Her gaze narrowed. "We're both paying."

It wasn't a question. Based on the set of her jaw, she wouldn't give in. With three older siblings, he'd learned to pick his battles early in life. "Okay."

Saying that, however, only brought a bitter cough syrup taste to his mouth. No matter what Sheridan believed, they weren't in the same situation. Not even close. He would have millions—hundreds of millions—in the bank, and she would need to find a job and a place to live.

But he couldn't tell her the truth. If he wouldn't share the news with his family, how could he tell a near-stranger?

Besides, she'd never know, anyway. He had no reason to feel guilty.

"Now…" She rubbed her palms together, looking cute in her faded jeans, oversized sweater, and suede boots. "Let's find the perfect Christmas tree."

Her enthusiasm was a one-eighty from how she'd acted at the coffee shop yesterday. Today, she appeared lighter. It pleased him to know he'd played a part in that. "You pick the tree."

Her smile disappeared, leaving parted lips in its place. "I thought we were doing this together."

"We are." The words rushed out. He'd do anything to light up her pretty face again. "But you're better suited to be the tree picker. Me? I'm a pro at carrying heavy stuff to cars."

The corners of her mouth tugged upward. "Teamwork."

"Yes, teamwork."

For two strangers, they made a good team. Yesterday, while Sheridan checked out more of the shops on Main Street, he'd returned to the house and brought in the boxes of decorations Von had left. They'd fixed their own dinners but ate together, discussing their favorite shows, movies, and music. They didn't have as much in common with those, but that made it more fun. This morning, she'd stayed in her bedroom until it was time for lunch. Funny, but he'd missed having breakfast with her.

"So, any preferences? Thin or bushy, short or tall?"

"I defer to your expertise, but it has to fit in or on my SUV. But don't let the pressure get to you."

"No worries." She surveyed the rows of trees. "I've done this many times. You're looking at an expert tree-picker."

She was attractive, but her confidence appealed to him at a gut level. "Excellent, because I spoke to my mom this morning. She wants me to send her a pic once the tree is up."

"That's funny. My mom said the same thing to me."

"Can't disappoint the moms."

"Nope, but thankfully mine is easy to please." Affection filled her voice.

"You're close to her."

"She's the best. I mean, she has her moments, as any mom does, but she's so devoted to me, Max, and the rescue." Sheridan's gaze softened. "When I was younger, I accused her of loving the animals more than me. Now, I realize animals often face life-and-death situations, and that must be her priority. That doesn't mean I come second or don't matter as much."

"Your mom sounds like a special person."

With a nod, Sheridan headed to the first row of trees.

He would have enjoyed hearing more about her mom, but this probably wasn't the best time, given how fast Sheridan moved.

She glanced over her shoulder, her eyes bright and a wide grin on her face. "Are you coming?"

"Walk, don't run. Or you'll set a bad example for the kids."

"I'm not running." She stuck out her tongue at him. "I'm hurrying. We don't want someone else to end up with our tree."

"If that happens, then it wasn't meant to be ours."

"Philosophy major?"

"Social media quote. I can't remember what platform."

She laughed.

He caught up with her. The row had Noble firs, but he'd noticed Douglas firs when they parked. "Do you have a favorite tree?"

"Not really. My mom has her favorite, but I've always just picked one I've liked. How about you?"

"My mom always gets a Douglas fir. My sister Madison is all about Nobles. For me, a tree is a tree. Put some lights and decorations on one, and they all look nice."

"Good to know you're not picky." As she peered around a tree, her gaze narrowed. "I'm spoiled with trees. In Berry Lake, we get a permit and cut our own."

"In the forest?"

"Yes, but there are local farms you can visit, if you prefer to do that."

"Sounds fun."

"It's a tradition in my family. Well, my mom's side now." Sheridan moved on to another tree. "We got ours two weeks ago. Snow flurries were coming down. It was almost…"

Michael noticed she didn't mention her father and hadn't since their visit to Sweet Caroline's Café yesterday. He wouldn't bring up the loser. The guy didn't deserve a daughter like Sheridan. "What?"

A wistful expression crossed Sheridan's face. "Magical. That was the only Christmassy thing I've done this year until now."

"We don't have snow, but a coastal Christmas can be just as nice as a white one."

She glanced his way. "I can't wait."

Neither could he. "I'm honored you're celebrating with me."

Sheridan smirked playfully. "You should be."

Before he could say anything, she continued along the row. She ran her fingers along the branch of a tree. "This is already dry. We should get a fresher one, so needles don't end up all over Von and Hope's place."

"We also don't want to bring in a fire hazard. Marley would never forgive me."

"Hope and Von might not like it, either."

"The ones you cut yourself must be super fresh."

She nodded. "But one time, we ended up with hundreds of baby spiders."

He shivered. "Talk about a nightmare before Christmas."

"Not a fan of spiders?"

"Nope." And they also weren't something he wanted to discuss. "Do you yell 'timber' when it falls?"

"Of course. That's part of the tradition, but someone holds on to it, so the branches don't break."

She'd mentioned tradition before. That gave Michael an idea. "Do you have a lot of Christmas ones?"

"A few, like cutting our Christmas tree and drinking hot spiced apple cider while we decorate it."

"We can pick some up at the store if you'd like."

She stopped. "That would be great. I mean if you don't mind."

"I don't." He spied a squat, bushy tree. The thing was as tall as it was wide. Not for him, but someone would love it. "Traditions are important. What are some of the others you do?"

"Bake cookies." She checked out a tall, thin tree. "My grandparents were German. My grandma enjoyed celebrating Yuletide. She'd make these yummy cookies. The entire house would smell like them."

"We should make them."

"You bake?"

He shrugged. "How hard can cookies be?"

"True. I'll ask my mom to email me the recipe." She headed to a shorter tree. "We always have lasagna on Christmas Eve, and then we attend midnight Mass. How about you?"

"We spend Christmas Eve at one of my aunts' houses. She makes ham and turkey. Christmas dinner is at my parents' house, and my mom serves prime rib." He might have to up his plans for those two dinners. Maybe order takeout if any restaurants were open. "Our big family tradition is making ornaments. Even though we're all adults, my mom still makes us do it. She puts up all the ornaments each year, even the ones we made when we were toddlers."

"That's a lovely tradition."

"It is, but we'd never admit it to her." He laughed. "My brother, Mason, complains the loudest, but he also takes the most pride in his creations. He made one for his son, who is celebrating his first Christmas this year."

"We should each make an ornament. I'm sure there's a dollar store that would have some craft stuff."

"That's a great idea. We can leave them for Von and Hope as a thank-you gift for letting us stay at the cottage."

"That's sweet."

Michael flashed her his most charming smile. "I can be as sweet as you want me to be. Even sweeter than Caroline's pies."

One side of Sheridan's mouth lifted. "That's quite a claim."

His gaze locked on hers. "You'll see."

The words hung in the air as if suspended between them, and Michael didn't want to disturb it. He waited for her to look away, but she didn't. He was in no hurry to break the connection he felt with her. Something seemed to hold them together. An invisible cable or a current of some sort.

Whatever it was, he didn't want it to end.

"I need to go potty, Mommy!" a child yelled.

The sound jolted Michael from the daze he'd been in. He had no idea what had just happened. But it hadn't sucked. That should bother him more than it did.

He forced his gaze from Sheridan and laughed. "My nephew is still at the drool and goo stage, but it won't be long until he's like that kid."

"Do you enjoy being an uncle?"

As he imagined the baby, warmth flowed through him. "Monroe is the best little dude you've ever seen. The spit-up sucks if you don't have another shirt to change into, and dirty diapers can be nasty, but I love him."

She drew her eyebrows together. "You change diapers?"

"That's part of being an uncle." Her surprised expression made him laugh. He raised an eyebrow. "Surprised they trust me with their kid?"

"Shocked," Sheridan joked. "Seriously, it's great he has someone like you in his corner. All my relatives lived far away, so we rarely saw them. Aunts and uncles were people who sent Christmas cards or a check at graduation."

His extended family lived within an hour's drive to Charleston. "I can't imagine."

"Does it bother you to miss Monroe's first Christmas?" she asked.

"Not really. The little guy doesn't do much at his age, and his mom's family hasn't seen him as much as we have. And we'll get him next year, and I hope every Christmas after that."

She studied him.

He wiped his beard. "Do I have something on my face?"

"No, it's just…"

"What?"

"You sound more like a family man than a frat guy."

"My family means everything to me." Which was why Michael wanted to keep them safe. He counted down the days until he would tell them how their financial futures were now set.

"I can tell." Her gaze lingered before she focused on another tree. "We may need to try the next row."

"Or, you could close your eyes, spin, and pick whichever one you're facing."

Sheridan gasped. "Never. You can't just randomly pick a tree. That would be… wrong."

"It could be a new tradition to go along with our family ones."

She made a face. "We can come up with a better one than that."

At least she was game. "I'm sure we can."

"Oh." She went to the other side of the aisle. "This one has potential."

It looked like the others to him. "You're the boss."

"I want to pull it out to see the entire thing."

This was the first tree she'd been that interested in. "I'll…"

"I've got it." She pulled the tree free of the others with apparent ease.

He struck a pose. "I'll just stand here and look pretty."

Ignoring him, she circled the tree, ran her fingers along several branches, and checked the tag. Her face glowed. "This is the one."

Her choice surprised him. The tree was a little bare and lopsided. "Are you sure?"

"Positive."

"It's the one you want?"

"Yes." Her eyebrows drew together. "Do you want a different one?"

"No, it's your choice, but it's not…"

"What?"

"Perfect."

"It has bare spots and it's asymmetrical, but this tree has something the others don't."

He hoped not spiders. "What?"

"Character. If we position it right, no one will notice the flaws. And this one is half price."

Guilt slammed into him like a Clemson defensive lineman. "I can afford—"

"Don't say it." She smiled at the tree. "You said

it's my choice, and I pick this one."

At least it wasn't a Charlie Brown Christmas tree. More like a cousin, once removed. "Now it's my turn."

"Thank you." She stepped out of his way so he could pick it up. "If we didn't take this one, I doubt anyone else would And that would be a shame."

"It would be." But he doubted the tree cared.

She rubbed her hands together. "It's beautiful."

"Yes." Only he wasn't talking about the tree. It would look fine once it had lights and decorations on the branches. Sheridan was the beautiful one. Her cheeks were pink from the cold, and her eyes twinkled. His mouth went dry.

"Let's pay for this bad boy." He carried the tree to the pop-up tent.

A lady—Jingle according to her name tag—took off the price tag. "Do you need preservative, or tree food as I prefer to call it?"

"No, thanks," Sheridan replied before turning toward him. "My mom showed me what to use years ago. Something safe for the animals."

"Fine by me."

The other woman—Jangle—held up a cellophane-wrapped sprig of greenery. "We also have mistletoe."

His gaze shot to Sheridan's lips. Mistletoe might not be the smartest idea, except he remembered Von's list on the refrigerator.

"We'll take two."

"Two?" Sheridan repeated, wringing her hands.

"My mom hangs mistletoe in the house. Von also asked me to get some for the New Year's Eve party."

And if Michael caught Sheridan standing under a sprig, a kiss was simply... tradition.

9

At the beach cottage, the scent from the pot of hot spiced apple cider lingered in the air. Sheridan had found mulling spice bags at the market, which meant no cheesecloth required. The taste was a little different from home, but Michael drank three cups, so he must have enjoyed it.

"Carol of the Bells" came from the TV set. One channel played only music for the season. He said his mom listened to it.

As Sheridan put away the now-empty boxes of decorations, she hummed along to the song. She owed him a big thank-you. No way would skipping Christmas have been okay. Not when she relished the sights, sounds, and smells of the holiday. There might not be evergreen trees and snow outside the window, but the sand, grass, and the Atlantic Ocean were growing on her.

Michael placed a gold star on the top of the tree. "Is it straight?"

"Yes." Contentment filled her. "It's perfect."

"You said the tree would be, and it is. I should have never doubted you."

"You didn't put up much of a fight."

"No." He stared at the beautiful tree with twinkling white lights, shiny garland, and ornaments. "And I'm glad I didn't. This is the best tree."

Warm and fuzzy feelings surged through Sheridan. This wasn't the Christmas she thought she'd have, but it was the one she needed. "Thanks for suggesting we do this."

It had been strange hanging ornaments that held no memories for either of them, but she'd enjoyed seeing all the different ones, from colored balls to beach scenes painted by Hope. Sheridan and Michael had only disagreed on whether to add a strand of multicolor lights. After a five-minute stalemate, Michael pulled out a coin to decide. She'd won the toss, so they'd only put on the white bulbs—what she put on her tree. Well, used to, but she would again next year.

Wherever that might be.

But she didn't want to think about the future when she was enjoying the present so much.

"The white lights were the right choice."

Michael stepped away from the tree. "Now, to finish up."

Sheridan stared at the empty boxes. "There aren't any more decorations."

"Not the tree." He went to the breakfast bar and picked up the two packages of mistletoe. "We still have this."

"Oh." Sheridan had been trying to forget about those. Mistletoe hadn't been a tradition in either of her parents' houses. If her mom hung any this year, she hadn't noticed.

"Von left instructions." Michael moved toward the kitchen. "The nails are already there."

"Great." Her voice sounded flat.

Of course, it did. She didn't want to spend two weeks maneuvering around the mistletoe. Not that Michael wanted to kiss her. He'd made it clear this was about tradition. Not only his family's but the Ryan twins', too.

No big deal. Some greenery with berries was meaningless in the grand scheme of things. Too bad her lips hadn't keyed in on that point yet. All they wanted was a kiss.

Not. Going. To. Happen.

"Where do they go?" She'd meant to speak casually, but the words tumbled out of her mouth as if she were eager to find out and would loiter there.

Ugh. So not subtle, but she managed not to cringe. At least not outwardly.

"One goes in the space between the breakfast bar and the doorway."

She glanced that direction but didn't notice a nail. The spot, however, was prime for standing around during a party, which was probably the point. "And the other?"

"Outside on the deck."

That surprised her. "I wouldn't have guessed that."

"Me, either, except people go out there during parties." He unwrapped the mistletoe. "And I mean the lovebird couples, who need a break from the crowds to make out."

It must be nice.

Wait. What was she thinking?

Sheridan was in no position for a relationship with her life in upheaval. She had no idea what her address would be in a few weeks. Dating wasn't within the realm of possibility.

Too much hearth-and-home coziness doing holiday stuff with Michael was messing with her brain. She needed a distraction.

"I'll search for the nail." Sheridan stood between the wall and breakfast bar, but she didn't see it. She rose on her tiptoes and felt around the area. Her finger bumped into something. "I found it."

"Excellent. Being tall comes in handy."

"Except for when guys call you a giant because

they prefer petite women." The words spewed out—a habit. A lifetime of being teased made her defensive.

"I meant you don't have to worry about falling off a chair."

"That, too."

"But someone liking a different type doesn't justify name-calling."

"What's your type?"

His face reddened. "Short with blond hair."

Sheridan shouldn't be surprised. Many jocks liked that type. Even if he wasn't an athlete now, he must have been in the past. Still, disappointment shot through her. She shook it off. "People have types. It's not a big deal."

"It is if someone puts down another person. I wasn't doing that."

"I know. I'm just a bit…"

"Fragile?"

She nodded. "If my life weren't such a mess, I doubt I'd think twice about what you said. But things set me off more easily now."

"I get it." Michael held up the mistletoe tied with a red satin bow. "Check this out. Look at the berries and the red ribbon. This is better than what my mom buys. There's even a loop to hang it."

"The nail is next to where my finger is."

"Don't move."

Except the closer he came, the more the area

appeared to shrink. His warmth, his scent, his presence overwhelmed Sheridan. Each one of her nerve endings stood at alert, shouting *retreat*. Her throat tightened, and she swallowed. "Do you want me to get out of the way?"

"Not yet."

Figures.

The side of his arm grazed hers.

Tingles exploded at the point of contact. She needed to get away from him. "Do you see it?"

"I think so." He bumped against her again, and her pulse kicked up a notch. "Sorry."

"Take your time." That way, she had a few more minutes on this planet before she keeled over dead. Something about Michael Patterson slayed her. She didn't know if it was his friendliness or his hotness, but she would never survive being this close to him.

He raised the mistletoe, moving slowly toward the nail. "I've got it."

As relief washed over her, she lowered her hand and stepped aside. Who was she kidding? She returned to stack the rest of the empty boxes. If she hadn't moved, he might think she wanted a kiss. Okay, she wouldn't say no because... tradition. And a kiss would be nice.

Which told her the real issue—she didn't want to find out he didn't want to kiss her.

Pathetic.

Was she too old to run away? She'd sort of done that coming here. But her stay was temporary.

He hung the mistletoe. "What do you think?"

She was happy the mistletoe didn't talk because it would see right through her. "Easy enough to avoid."

Oh, no. She slapped a hand over her mouth. Had she said that aloud?

Michael laughed. "That's one way to look at it."

Heat rushed up to her neck. "It's also very Christmassy."

"Mistletoe is, but you're right." His grin made him more attractive. "It'll be easy to avoid here and on the deck."

He spoke smoothly, but hearing the words was difficult, even though she'd said something similar.

Disappointment tangled with relief. The odd combination told her to keep her distance from Michael. Not trusting her voice, she forced herself to nod.

"Now what?" he asked.

"We have dinner and enjoy the tree."

"What are you making?"

She removed the chicken from the fridge and took off the plastic wrapper. She would cook both breasts and save one for another day. "A salad with chicken."

"Healthier than my ramen noodles."

"I remember those days, which is why I no

longer eat it." However, she might have to reconsider, depending on her financial situation in a month or two.

"Easy and cheap, so it's a mainstay on my menu. Plus, my family needs something to kid me about."

"You provide the ammo?"

"Sometimes. Keeps things fresh that way."

She tried to imagine what his family was like, but she couldn't see past him. "I've never had to deal with that until the last few months."

"Has it been rough?"

Sheridan nodded. "I had no idea how bad it would be. My stepmother's kids are cruel. I haven't met all of them, but the youngest three are awful. Vicious. I wasn't in school at the same time as them, and I'm so glad. My stepfather's three daughters are nicer, but they still get on each other. So far, they've left me out of any sibling squabbles, and I hope that continues."

"When my siblings come after me, I dish back without a second thought."

"Wait." She remembered what he'd told her earlier. "You said you were a sweetie."

He waggled his eyebrows. "With the pretty ladies. My sisters don't count."

Did he consider her pretty? Sheridan's pulse spurted, and she stood taller. Until she thought about the context, and then she realized he hadn't meant her but ladies in general.

No biggie.

But it told her one thing. Time to call him out. "You talk tough, but I see right through your façade. Your sisters have you wrapped around their little finger as much as Monroe does."

Michael laughed, the deep sound circling Sheridan like her favorite wool scarf. "Okay, you got me. I'm not that tough with them. Some might say I'm a wimp. But with Mason, I don't let up and go at it with him."

The love in his voice for his siblings intensified the loneliness in Sheridan's heart. She had no way to change being an only child, but she would get to know Max's daughters better if she remained in Berry Lake.

She glanced at the clock. "It's getting late. I need to cook dinner. Do you want a chicken breast?"

Michael straightened. "Do you have extras?"

No, but she would buy more when she went to the market for the cookie ingredients. "Yes."

"I'd love one." He glanced at his stash of food. "If you want any ramen…"

"Thanks, but I'll pass." She removed the skillet from the cabinet, turned the dial to medium-high heat, and touched the button for the fan. The chicken wasn't quite at room temperature, but it was close enough. She seasoned the two pieces with salt and pepper before adding olive oil to the pan. "Four minutes on each side, and it'll be done."

"I'll get my ramen going." Once again, he took up most of the space, removing a saucepan from the cabinet.

She kept an eye on the chicken. "Tell me if I'm in your way."

"You're not." He set to work as if this were an *Iron Chef* competition, not just water heating. His serious expression amused her. He kept surprising her in good ways.

Not being his type was a blessing in disguise because she had a little crush on him. That explained why she reacted to him the way she did. She hadn't crushed on anyone in years, but it made sense because he'd helped her rediscover her Christmas spirit.

And if she was suddenly obsessed with the mistletoe hanging a few feet away from them, it didn't matter. They were roommates. They might end up as friends by the time she left Indigo Bay. But like ramen, kisses weren't on the menu.

Mistletoe or not.

* * *

The next day, Sheridan strolled along Main Street. She'd set off on her own because Michael had a few calls to make—most likely more interviews or his family—but she'd wanted to give him space, so she agreed to meet him later to buy the craft materials for their ornaments.

Not that she'd seen anything that would work other than Christmas-themed tissue paper, but he might be able to suggest other places to go.

She yawned, fighting the tiredness from a near-sleepless night. When she did sleep, a Christmas tree singing a love ballad with a sprig of mistletoe played a starring role in her dream. So had Michael.

The sign for the Chocolate Emporium beckoned. Chocolate contained caffeine, which would help her wake up. At least in theory. But she'd probably just get a sugar rush only to crash later and have the calories go straight to her hips.

"Sheridan," Michael called out.

She turned toward his voice.

Michael strode her way at a fast clip. He wore another baseball cap and had exchanged his hoodie for a sweater. He'd worn similar outfits before, but she kept staring at him.

He smiled. "I don't have your cell phone number, so I'm glad I found you."

"Me, too."

"Did you find any ornament stuff?"

"One possibility, but I wanted to see what else was out there before deciding."

"Coastal Creations has a class to paint ornaments."

The cost concerned her. Indigo Bay wasn't a cheap tourist trap, but a charming, small town that appealed to permanent residents and visitors. But if she mentioned money, Michael might offer to pay for her. She didn't want that to happen. "I'd rather make them ourselves. Isn't that your family tradition?"

"It is."

"Then, let's stick with the original plan."

"Okay, but do you mind a detour first?"

"Is there something you want to get?"

"I want to show you something." He led her down the block, opened a door, and motioned her inside.

She found herself surrounded by art. The lighting, the music, the smells... It was like coming home. Funny how she hadn't noticed this store when she was on Main Street yesterday. "What is this place?"

"Welcome to High Tide Gallery." A woman greeted them warmly. Her shoulder-length brown hair had a few silver strands mixed in. "I'm Melanie Bowers."

"I'm Sheridan DeMarco."

"Michael Patterson," he said.

"Patterson," Melanie repeated before tucking strands behind an ear. "Are you Marley's brother?"

"I am."

Melanie's smile widened. "I haven't worked

here long, but my fiancé, Penn, and I are friends with Von and Hope Ryan. They introduced us to your sister."

"Do you have any of Hope's work on display?" Sheridan asked, eager to see more of Hope's paintings.

"We do. Follow me." Melanie headed toward the back, passing by sculptures and other vignettes by artists. "We hope to get more of her works after she returns from her vacation."

Those must be the pieces Hope wanted Sheridan to catalog. She was halfway through them. She'd finished more this morning when sleep eluded her.

"She's a star on the rise." Sheridan did a double take at a large painting on the back wall Air rushed from her lungs. Her hand covered her heart. "Is that..."

"It's one of Hope's more recent works, and I love that she featured a sunset." Melanie motioned to the sold sticker. "It sold immediately, but the owners live in Nashville and aren't ready to take possession. We're happy to hold on to it since most people have a similar reaction to yours."

Sheridan could imagine. "I've never seen her use the purple and yellow hues in this way. The result is stunning."

"It is." Michael came forward to stand next to her. "I thought she was good, but this is beyond amazing."

"Sometimes Hope hides things in the paintings." Sheridan leaned forward. "Look closely, so you miss nothing."

"You're familiar with her work," Melanie said.

"I've seen a few of the pieces she's done in Berry Lake."

"She mentioned a show there in February."

"Yes." Sheridan didn't want to talk about the gallery or Sal, but she hoped the exhibit happened. It would be a massive boon for business.

"I should return to the front. Just call my name if you need help." Mischief gleamed in Melanie's eyes. "And in case you didn't notice, the two of you are standing under the mistletoe ball."

With that, she walked away.

Mistletoe!

Please don't let it be true.

Sheridan was afraid to look, but she did. Her heart dropped, straight to her feet. If not for her boots, it might have kept going.

The ball hung from a green velvet ribbon. She could almost hear it mocking her and her silly crush. Okay, not really. But the voice in her head wouldn't shut up.

Michael glanced at the ceiling. "I didn't notice that."

"Me, either. But we—"

"It's tradition to kiss under the mistletoe," he

interrupted. "If you refuse, it's bad luck."

"Right. I can't afford more of that."

"Then we'll just do a peck."

Heat pooled in her cheeks. "Fine."

What else could she say, especially with her heart playing its rendition of "The Little Drummer Boy"?

They met halfway, not moving their lower bodies, only the upper part. Their lips barely touched, but then someone moved closer. She didn't know if it was him or her, but the brush of lips turned into a full-on kiss. A hot, make-her-blood-boil kiss she didn't want to end. Only their mouths touched, but that was enough.

Who was she kidding?

His kiss was everything.

A bell rang.

The front door.

They weren't alone. They were in the...

Gallery.

She jerked back, inhaling deeply. Thankfully, her lungs remembered to breathe after being kissed so thoroughly. "No bad luck for us."

He stuck his fingertips in his pocket. "None at all."

Sheridan wasn't sure if she should be upset or relieved that this was no big deal to him when her heart continued to race like the speed boats on Berry Lake. Words failed her, but she needed to say something—anything. "Thanks for showing me the gallery."

"You're welcome." He glanced at the man and woman speaking to Melanie. "We should go find stuff to make ornaments."

"Okay." And get far, far away from the mistletoe ball. At least she knew where it hung at the beach house. Her lips wanted another taste of Michael, but that wouldn't happen again.

Otherwise, her crush might turn into something else.

10

With a baseball cap on, Michael stood in the baking aisle of the local market, staring at Sheridan as she compared two bags of brown sugar. He couldn't turn back time, but an hour or even forty-five minutes would be enough to put them at the High Tide Gallery again. Instead of agreeing they wouldn't have bad luck and walking out, as if nothing had happened under the mistletoe ball, he would say more about their kiss.

He wanted to do that now, but something held him back—the same way it had at the gallery.

On their walk along Main Street.

Inside the drugstore.

And now at the market.

Based on his sisters, women made a big deal about mistletoe kisses. To be honest, they'd always been a joke to him, a nudge-nudge kind of thing between him and his friends. At least they had been until today.

Now he was rethinking... everything.

Including his *type*.

Tall, leggy, and brunette with full kissable lips and breathy sighs suddenly appealed to him in a way he'd never imagined. The same way Sheridan's kiss affected him differently from every other before hers.

Was he losing his mind or lonely from not dating?

Whatever the reason, he needed it to stop.

Now.

He blamed himself for this situation.

Why should Sheridan mention the kiss when he'd shaken it off, acted like it was no big deal, and tried to forget about it?

That might be what guys did. Well, what *he* did.

Unfortunately, he'd only accomplished two of the three. Her kiss was branded on his lips. She hadn't been unaffected. It had taken time for her pupils to return to their normal size and her breathing to become less shallow. Her cheeks, however, remained pinker than usual.

From walking to the various stores or because of kissing him?

Michael hoped the latter. Call him selfish, but he didn't like being the only one caught up in this...

whatever it was he thought about her. He barely knew her, so it wasn't the F-word—feelings.

She placed one bag of brown sugar in the basket. There shouldn't be much difference between the packages, but how she studied the labels was cute. "We only need honey and molasses."

"The honey should be with the peanut butter, but I don't have a clue about molasses." He'd never used that. At least not knowingly.

"I know where they are," she said, not missing a beat.

He followed her, trying to think of a way to ask her if the kiss was a one-off or if she wanted more.

Direct would be best.

But that wasn't like him.

Soon, they had the two items.

"We're all set to make the cookies." She lowered her phone. "Do you need anything?"

More kisses, but those didn't appear to be on her list.

Just talk to her.

Or, he could sleep under the mistletoe to see if she'd kiss him when she woke.

Grow up.

Stop acting like a twelve-year-old.

You're not Mikey. You're Michael.

Don't be that guy.

Talk to her.

His sisters' voices filled his head. He didn't disagree with any of those things, but he preferred the path of least resistance. And twelve had been an awesome age.

"Michael?" Sheridan asked.

"What?" She must have been talking to him. "I'm sorry. I didn't hear you."

"Freshly made pizzas are on sale for ten dollars. Do you want to split one for dinner?"

"I never say no to pizza."

"Meat lovers, pepperoni, cheese, or veggie?"

"Pepperoni."

"My favorite." She placed it in the cart. "I have salad, too."

"Sounds good." Sheridan had fed him last night. He would provide something, too. He grabbed a box of chocolate-covered cherries. "How about these for dessert? They're another family tradition. No matter whose house we visit, everyone has these."

She laughed. "My mom buys them, too."

He placed them in the basket and handed her a twenty-dollar bill. They'd decided to split the expenses for any Christmas tradition. But his guilt continued to rise each time she pulled out her wallet.

This morning, Michael's team had told him the date they would redeem his ticket—January seventh. That had made the situation more real.

As they exited the market, Sheridan grinned. "Thank you for hanging out with me today."

"You're welcome. I had fun."

"Me, too."

This was his chance. He wasn't one for talking. Mason had taught him actions spoke louder than words. Still, Michael took a breath and blew it out. "So, the kiss at the gallery…"

"The mistletoe ball was pretty."

Not where he was going with this, but at least she hadn't shut him down. "Yes, but are you okay?"

Her nose crinkled. "With what?"

"The kiss." The word shot out. "I mean, I don't want you to be weirded out since we're sharing the house."

"Do you feel weird?"

"No."

"I don't, either."

Okay, they were talking, but they weren't getting anywhere. "I enjoyed it."

"Me, too."

He debated asking if they could try it at home under the mistletoe there, but he decided against it. "So, we're good?"

"Of course." She sounded nonchalant. "Mistletoe is a tradition. No different from the cookies we'll bake tomorrow or the ornaments we'll make on the twenty-third."

Her calm tone bristled. "Right."

Except it seemed wrong.
Wrong. Wrong. Wrong.
Only, what could he do about it?

* * *

The next day, kissing Sheridan remained on Michael's mind. Maybe he needed to go on a date or kiss someone. Someone who wasn't his roommate. He crawled out of bed, just in time to answer a call from one of his team who wanted him to check his inbox.

He did, only to find a hundred attachments—okay, more like ten—they asked him to read and sign. The documents had nothing to do with winning the lottery. No, these were things most responsible adults had, like a will, advanced medical directive, durable power of attorney, medical power of attorney, and letter of intent. He typed a note into his phone to make sure his parents and siblings had all this stuff, too.

After promising to return everything before Christmas, he hung up. He hadn't slept well, so caffeine might help. He put on a T-shirt and trudged to the kitchen.

No sign of Sheridan, unfortunately, and the mistletoe appeared to mock him, but a pot of fresh coffee waited for him. He would call it a win.

He poured himself a cup. The hot liquid slid down his throat.

No dishes filled the sink, but that didn't mean Sheridan hadn't eaten. She enjoyed walks along the beach, even though he'd yet to take one. He grabbed a pouch with two strawberry Pop-Tarts in it and returned to his room. They planned to bake cookies at eleven, so he had time to read the some of the documents.

He digested the beneficiary form as easily as his breakfast. After signing it, he uploaded the document into his lawyer's portal. The next one, however, was longer, and the legalese made his brain hurt. By the fourth page, the words blurred.

He rubbed his tired eyes. It was only ten o'clock, but a nap might re-energize him.

His cell phone rang. His mom's name showed on the screen. "Hey, Mom."

"Hello, Mikey. Sorry I didn't call yesterday, but your grandfather's gout flared up, so we tried to distract him."

His grandpa was a big guy. Everyone said Michael took after him. "Is he better today?"

"Yes." His mom chuckled. "Sometimes, I think he plays up his symptoms for attention."

Michael wouldn't put it past the tough-as-nails man who'd fought in the Korean War and was a former Golden Gloves boxing champion but turned into a giant puppy dog around his grandchildren. "At ninety, he's allowed to do whatever he wants to do."

"That's what your grandma said. Your tree is beautiful. Did your girlfriend help you decorate?"

He scrubbed his face. "No."

"Did Sheridan help? That's the name of the woman who's also staying at the beach cottage with you, right?"

Ugh. Von must have mentioned it to Marley, who told their mom and most likely everyone else. "Yes, Sheridan helped. And she's not staying with me. We're sharing the place."

"I thought you had help with the tree."

"Decorating a Christmas tree doesn't require a special degree or a subscription to one of those home magazines you read or a feminine touch." His mom was old-school. She still used a paper calendar and subscribed to magazines. And okay, he'd never put up his own tree before, but that didn't mean he couldn't.

"Does she get along with your girlfriend?" His mom's curiosity dripped from each word.

"It's just Sheridan and me here."

"Oh, honey. I'm sorry." His mom's tone was soft and caring. "Was your girlfriend upset to have someone else there? Is it over or something you can work through?"

It amazed Michael how people made assumptions and formed stories about someone else's life. "I'm fine. There's nothing to work out."

Both things were true. And he hoped that

would stop the questions about his nonexistent girlfriend.

As soon as he hung up with his mom, Mason called. Then Madison. And finally, Marley. His family had made today *National Bug Michael Day*. Not that he minded talking with them, but he wanted to help make cookies. Hours later, he finally said goodbye to his sister. He showered and dressed before heading to the living room.

Sheridan sat on the couch, staring at her phone. She glanced up. "Hey."

"I'm so sorry to be late. My family called."

"It's not a problem. Family should always come first."

Michael nodded. He smelled the pine from the Christmas tree, but something was missing. "You haven't baked the cookies?"

"We're sharing our traditions. I wanted to wait for you."

His throat clogged with emotion. "Thanks for waiting. Do you want to make them now?"

She glanced at her phone. "Would you mind if we waited until later? I want to go to the animal rescue's Adoption and Christmas Fair."

It wasn't an invitation, but a question gleamed in her eyes. Hope, too.

Michael hesitated. He'd already been out and about more than he planned. A few people had recognized him, not as the mysterious blurry lottery winner from the convenience store but as Von Ryan's future brother-in-law. His attorney had forwarded a recent article questioning the ethics of outing a winner entitled to remain anonymous. Not that people had stopped, but that was in Charleston, not Indigo Bay. Another trip out shouldn't be an issue. "Mind if I tag along?"

Her face lit up—the result breathtaking. "I'd love the company."

"It's a date." He cringed. "I mean…"

She touched his arm. "Don't worry about it. I know what you mean."

Did she? Because he wasn't sure why part of him wished it could be more. "Let me put on some shoes, and then we can go."

* * *

The Indigo Bay Animal Rescue's Adoption and Christmas Fair was held at the community center. Whereas the Barks and Bows Gala had been fancy, this event was down-home with hand-cut snowflakes hanging from the ceiling, tables sponsored by various civic groups, crafters, and shops, and animals—lots and lots of them. Dogs, cats, and an iguana waited with their families to have a photo with a jolly Santa Claus.

A few dogs wore "Adopt Me" vests. Their wagging tails and happy faces suggested they enjoyed being there. Some cats, however, meowed in their crates. Others pawed between the grating to get the attention of people passing by.

But the best thing in the place was Sheridan's smile.

"This is wonderful." She pulled out her phone and took photos. "Look at the crowd. They should be able to adopt out some animals and raise more money."

"Where do you want to start?" he asked.

"I have no idea."

"You should buy an ornament for the community tree. They're non-breakable and perfect for making wishes on and hanging outdoors. Plus, the money goes to a good cause." An older woman with perfectly coiffed hair, false eyelashes, and heavy makeup stood in front of them. Her forest-green dress had candy cane buttons. A small white dog, wearing a collar that matched the woman's green heels, pranced at her feet. "The gala was a success, but it didn't raise enough to cover the expansion. It'll be up to this little event to make up the difference."

"Thanks for telling us." Sheridan extended her hand. "I'm Sheridan DeMarco."

"Lucille Sanderson." She shook hands but then eyed Sheridan warily. "You're not from around here."

"Washington State."

Lucille rolled her eyes. "One of those tree hugger granola types. Well, your money is as good as anyone else's."

Michael bit back a laugh. He'd heard stories about this woman from Von and Marley but thought they were urban legends.

"And who are you?" Lucille's gaze narrowed. "You look vaguely familiar."

"I'm Michael Patterson. Von Ryan is engaged to my sister, ma'am."

"Let's hope you're not as flakey as your sister. She broke poor Von's heart." Lucille glanced at her dog. "Remember when that happened, Princess? You needed to cheer him up."

The woman was too much. Michael couldn't wait to tell Marley about this. "I'm sure Princess was a big help. And thankfully, my sister realized her mistake."

"A good thing, because a man like Von wouldn't have been on the market long." Lucille clucked her tongue. "It's been nice meeting you. Princess needs her photo taken with Santa, and I want a photo with that handsome actor Eric Slade, so I'll leave you to spend your money."

"How much does the rescue still need to raise?" Sheridan asked.

"Twenty-three thousand dollars," Lucille answered. "But Christmas is a time for miracles. Goodbye."

With that, the woman hurried away, leaving a trail of perfume in her wake.

Sheridan stared after her. "Ms. Sanderson is..."

"A well-known busybody in Indigo Bay."

"At least she's here to support a good cause." Sheridan surveyed the fair. "We never talked about going to the community tree lighting on Christmas Eve. We could buy the ornaments she mentioned to use."

"That sounds like a plan. Who knows what else we'll find?"

"I want to help the rescue reach its goal." Emotion filled Sheridan's voice. "Vet bills are never-ending but then to expand a building... That's a huge undertaking. So many rescues run in the red, and others end up bankrupt. Sometimes, the founders use their own money to keep things going."

"Is that what your mom does?"

"She has in the past, which was an issue with my dad. He claims the rescue was the reason for their divorce." Sheridan smiled at a medium-sized dog who walked with his head held high as if proud to be wearing the adoption vest. "Animal rescue is a passion for those involved, including the volunteers. There are heartaches, tears, and happy endings, but most can't imagine doing anything else. My mom doesn't have an event like this, but she runs a Home for the Holidays program where people temporarily foster an animal. Not everyone adopts, a handful do, but the animals are in a home over Christmas."

"You love animals."

She nodded. "My father was all about art. My mom threw herself into animal rescue. Both mean a lot to me."

"Do you have any pets?"

"No, I lived in an apartment and worked during the day. My mom has so many she doesn't need me bringing more there. Someday, I'll have one."

"You have plenty of time."

"That's what I keep telling myself."

Michael fought the urge to wrap his arms around Sheridan and tell her he'd make sure she would be okay. The uncertainty in her life must suck. But he could do something.

Two things, actually.

"What's your mom's rescue called?" he asked.

"Berry Lake Animal Rescue," Sheridan answered without a second thought. "She considered making it more cutesy like Whiskers and Wags or Purrs and Paws, but the name she picked gets the job done."

"Let's find the ornaments, and then we can see what else they have."

As they stood in line, Michael made a note of her mom's rescue and the Indigo Bay one. Then, he sent a text to his attorney.

Me: *I want to donate to two animal rescues. $25K*

each. Can you make that happen?

JD$: *If you had the money.*

Me: *Haha, but I'm serious. Is there any way?*

JD$: *A pledge with a payable or funding date in January. It would have to be anonymous.*

Me: *Do it.*

JD$: *Are you sure?*

Me: *Positive.*

JD$: *Send me the exact names and locations, and I'll take care of it.*

Me: *Thanks.*

JD$: *Must admit, you've surprised me with this one.*

Me: *Thought I'd want a fast car and a beautiful woman first?*

JD$: *Yes.*

Michael nearly laughed. *Me, too.* But he'd made the right choice.

Me: *I finally understand what you guys have been trying to explain about the money and how it's not only about living comfortably and helping my family and friends. I can make a big difference in other places, too.*

JD$: *Yes, and this is an excellent start. I'll be in touch.*

Sheridan would never know who made the donation or that he'd done this for her. And funnily enough, that was the best feeling in the world, and he wanted to do it more.

For her and others.

11

On the walk from the community center, Sheridan focused on the sidewalk in front of her. She'd stared enough at Michael. He hadn't caught her yet, and she wanted to keep it that way. At least he couldn't see into her daydreams—ones involving a ceiling covered in mistletoe. His kiss was that good.

"The fair was fun." He walked next to her, shortening his stride slightly to match hers. "And more my style than the gala."

"Mine, too." She raised the bag containing two ornaments for the community tree and three dog toys she'd purchased to donate to her mom's rescue. "Unlike the auction, we could afford to do our part at the fair. Let's hope everyone else does theirs."

"Lots of people were buying things. They should reach their goal." Michael nudged her with his shoulder. "I saw you stick dollar bills into the donation bin. You could have used that money to take a selfie with Eric Slade."

She shrugged. The actor was older but gorgeous. "I enjoy his movies, but I'm not the starstruck type."

"You seemed taken by that terrier."

"Puppy dog eyes get me every time."

"That's why I'm still surprised you don't have a pet."

Sheridan felt a pang in her heart. She should tell him the truth. "I would have had one, except Sal said no pets in the apartment. I think it was his way of getting revenge on my mom for the animals she had during their marriage. But someday, I want a dog and a cat."

Michael raised an eyebrow. "Only one of each?"

"To start."

He laughed. "That's what I figured."

She stopped at the corner. Cars and trucks whizzed by on Seaside Boulevard. A good thing there was a traffic light, or they'd be players in a real-life video game with high stakes. There hadn't been this many cars before, but it was late afternoon, so maybe this was rush hour in Indigo Bay.

Michael hit the crosswalk button. "I've never

been to anything like that before. To be honest, I didn't know they existed."

"The rescue did a wonderful job. There was something for everyone."

"Like the little girl who brought her goldfish to see Santa."

"That was so cute. I enjoyed seeing people buy the pre-filled stockings for dogs and cats." Most of all, Sheridan loved seeing the people filling out adoption forms. Even if folks didn't get a dog or cat at the fair, there were probably more at the rescue's kennel. "I sent my mom the photos and can't wait to hear what she says."

"Do you think she'll organize an event like that?"

"Maybe. She's got so much going on, and now that she's remarried, she's training more volunteers, so she doesn't have to do everything. The weather in December can be iffy. A snowstorm can cancel events. July or August would be a better time because of the number of tourists in town."

"Summer is a big draw?"

She nodded. "The Huckleberry Festival and Bigfoot Seeker Gathering are huge draws."

He shook his head. "Bigfoot?"

"Bigfoot is a big deal in Berry Lake. There's a guide. He and his sons take people out on Sasquatch hunts."

Michael's face lit up. "Have you gone on one?"

"No, it's for tourists who enjoy hiking, camping, wearing night-vision goggles." And wasting money, in her opinion.

"That sounds so cool—a bucket list item."

Really? She'd never been interested, but she might be jaded, growing up hearing all the Bigfoot stories. "You should come to Berry Lake and go on one of their trips."

His gaze locked with hers. "If I do, you can show me around town."

Her heart stumbled. Whenever he looked at her, Sheridan felt herself falling down a rabbit hole. Worse? She didn't mind at all.

And that worried her.

The same way she kept thinking about his lips.

His kiss.

"Uh, sure." She'd been playing it cool, when inside, she was flailing. Every smile or touch of his made her want to write a new set of rules to replace the ones they were no longer following. Rules that called for mistletoe kisses, holding hands, and cuddling on the couch. She forced herself to focus on him. "But night-vision goggles aren't required for my tour."

"That's okay. I'll wear them when I search for Bigfoot."

His grin might as well have been a roman candle. It ignited a fire in her stomach.

Oh, boy. She needed rules to keep her away from him.

Her crush was growing. That had to stop.

Anything else, including more kisses, wouldn't be smart. They were both unemployed. They lived in different states on opposite coasts. They had no idea what the new year would bring. And the biggest reason of all—she wasn't his type.

Sheridan could change the color of her hair—not that she would do that for a guy—but she was stuck with her height and build.

Not that either of them was in any position to get involved. But his kiss suggested he might be up for something more.

Something casual.

Part of her wished she were up for the same thing. She prided herself on being strong, but a person could only handle so much, and she'd had enough after Thanksgiving. A holiday romance or whatever one called it would only end up breaking her heart.

The light changed, and they crossed the road.

"So, time to bake cookies?" he asked.

"Yes. It won't take long if you also want to make the ornaments."

"Let's save those for tomorrow. We can turn on a holiday movie tonight. That's something my family does. Lifetime, Hallmark, Netflix. The choice is yours."

She did a double take. No way was this possible. "You'll watch without being forced?"

He nodded.

She placed her free hand against his forehead. "You don't have a temperature."

He laughed. "It's a tradition."

"True, but my stepfather, Max, threatened to cancel cable after my mom and stepsister binged on the Hallmark Channel."

Michael's jaw jutted forward. "Where were you?"

"Packing for this trip."

"You were in the skipping-Christmas mode."

Busted. Sheridan nodded. "I was doing well at it until you."

"Someday, you'll thank me."

"I already have."

"We're watching a movie tonight. You have to catch up."

"They repeat. There's also Christmas in July."

"That's too far away. And I prefer to celebrate in December. So cookies and movies."

The plural caught her attention. "Why not?"

* * *

The dough for the lebkuchen cookies needed to chill in the refrigerator for two hours, so they settled down for a movie. It featured a holiday decorator and a businessman whose family was visiting for Christmas. It was cute. They each sat on one side of the couch. The space between them was noticeable—to her, at least.

Don't think about it.

But watching the movie couple fall in love made her want that to happen to her and Michael. At least there wasn't much kissing until the end. Otherwise, she might want to reposition the mistletoe over him.

The next film was set at the Plaza in New York, and Sheridan loved seeing the grand hotel.

The timer rang.

"The dough is ready." She rose. "I'll preheat the oven."

"What about the movie?"

Maybe he was a romantic at heart. She'd stopped making assumptions about him because whenever she did, they turned out wrong. "We can do both if we make cookies during the commercials?"

"That's a perfect plan."

She sat.

At the next break, they ran into the kitchen. She preheated the oven, pulled the dough from the fridge, and covered the cookie sheet with parchment paper. "We have two batches to make since I had enough ingredients. I'll show you what to do, and you can do the other one."

He glanced around the corner. "Still a commercial, so what do we do?"

Sheridan enjoyed hearing him say "we." She grabbed a handful of flour. "Add flour to the cutting board and use a rolling pin to flatten the dough into a rectangular shape."

"Sounds easy."

She demonstrated. "It is."

"The movie's on."

They raced to the couch, and she made sure she touched nothing. Otherwise, there would be flour everywhere. At the next commercial break, they returned to the kitchen.

She finished rolling the dough.

He leaned forward. "That looks close enough."

Sheridan laughed. "Go watch the movie."

"No way." He pressed against her back, sending her pulse skyrocketing. "We're doing this together. Besides, I saw this one last year with Madison when Rory was out of town. What's the next step?"

"Grab a knife and cut the dough into smaller rectangles." She glanced at her phone. "My mom says there should be around eighteen."

"Geometry lessons via baking."

She shivered. "No math talk, please. Calculators and cash registers work fine."

He wagged his finger. "You're playing into the stereotype of the liberal arts major."

"I embrace it fully."

"Duly noted." He counted the cookies. "Twenty."

"More for us to eat." She placed the pieces on the cookie sheet and then washed her hands. "Now, we put them in the oven and wait."

The pan slid onto the middle rack, and she closed the door.

"Come on. The movie's starting." He grabbed her hand. "I want you to see the ugly sweaters his family wears."

Michael led her to the couch and pulled her down next to him on the sofa. Forget the space that was between them before. His thigh pressed against hers. He hadn't let go of her hand, either.

No big deal. Still, she forced herself to breathe.

Finally, he let go.

She missed his warmth and fought the urge to flex her fingers.

"This is like my family minus the sweaters. The men are all about Christmas ties. Except for Uncle Guy. He goes for holiday socks. It used to be boxers, but Great-Aunt Tessie stopped that."

Good for his great-aunt. Sheridan waited for a break in the movie's dialogue. "These relatives are on the Patterson side?"

"Yes." Michael's arm went over the back of the sofa. "Good people. There's a group chat, and everyone is trying to outdo each other with their holidays this year."

Another commercial came on. As she angled toward him, her shoulder slipped under his as if they were matching puzzle pieces.

"Who's winning?" she asked.

"So far, it's a tie between my cousin Elijah and my uncle Tim." Michael's affectionate tone told her how much he cared for his extended family. "One won a car playing slots in Atlantic City, and the other got to be on the sideline for the Panthers game, but there's time before New Year's for someone to pull ahead. Most of the Pattersons are competitive, whereas most of the Evans family are go-with-the-flow types."

"I'm not sure how you keep everybody straight."

"Once you reach a certain age, you learn to answer to *hey, you*." His hand rested on her shoulder. He stiffened before moving his arm to his side.

"I'm sorry." He sounded surprised and contrite. "I don't know what I was—"

A noise blared.

Sheridan stiffened. It was coming from the kitchen. "The cookies."

She bolted from the couch.

Smoke filled the air.

Michael opened windows and then turned off the smoke detector. "Are there flames?"

"Not that I can see."

He put on a nearby oven mitt. "Stand back."

Slowly, he opened the door. More smoke poured out. He removed the cookie tray and placed it on the stovetop. Each rectangle was black, scorched from baking much longer than needed.

She hung her head. "It's my fault. I forgot to turn on the timer."

"No. I'm the one who pulled you away before you could do that."

"I should have remembered."

He raised her chin with his finger. "Cookies aren't something you can multitask."

"I had the recipe from my mom, yet I ruined this tradition."

"You were distracted," he countered. "And so was I."

"The TV…"

"It wasn't the movie."

Sheridan's gaze met his, and her lips parted.

Before she could say anything, he kissed her. It didn't matter that smoke rose from the cookies and still hung in the air, and the smoke detector emitted a random beep. The only thing that she cared about was his lips against hers. She might care later. Who was she kidding? She would, but at this moment, she wanted to enjoy the taste and feel of him.

His beard brushed against her chin. She wrapped her arms around his neck, weaving her fingers through his hair. As she moved her hands down his shoulders, her palms ran along the muscular ridges. He was solid and kissing her senseless. She wanted the kiss to keep going.

His arms circled Sheridan, pulling her against him. She went willingly, eager to be closer.

She may have ruined the cookies, but she was nailing their kiss and didn't want it to end.

But then he eased away.

A whimper sounded. It had been her. That was enough to make her move back.

Sheridan glanced at the ceiling. The mistletoe was at least five feet from them.

He tucked strands of hair behind her ear. "I've wanted to do that since the art gallery."

"Me, too, but you didn't say anything."

"Neither did you." He laughed. "We're a pair."

She nodded. "We have to work on our cookie baking, but we're not hopeless. We've got the kissing down."

"We might need more practice."

"There's more cookie dough in the fridge."

"I meant practice kissing."

"Oh."

He brushed his mouth over hers. "We're also missing the rest of the movie."

"Yes, but we're living our own right here. No doubt, it's destined to be a classic."

Michael traced her lips with his fingertip. "Tell me more."

"Two strangers in a charming small town for Christmas share a quaint beach cottage. They both want to get away and be alone for the holidays, but there's nowhere else for one of them to stay."

"That sounds vaguely familiar."

Sheridan nodded. "At first, she thinks he's nothing but a frat party guy."

His eyes widened. "And he thinks she's uptight and will be in his way all the time."

She raised her chin. "Uptight?"

"Frat party guy?"

They both laughed.

Michael grinned. "She gets in the way, but he doesn't mind."

"He proves himself useful by helping her with a painting and suggests they celebrate Christmas."

"She finds them a perfect tree." He bit his lip. "And she makes him chicken."

"He takes her into an art gallery and kisses her under the mistletoe."

"But they haven't rescued an animal or saved the town."

"No, but they"—she glanced at the cookie sheet—"keep the cottage from burning down."

"The movie is missing something." Michael cupped her face and kissed her. "That's better."

"I'm sure we just exceeded the number of kisses for Hallmark."

"Bring on Lifetime or Netflix," he joked. "So, what happens next?"

She smiled, unsure of what was happening between them, but happy enough that she didn't want to think about it right now. "We'll have to wait and see."

"I thought you might say something like that." He opened the refrigerator and pulled out the rest of the cookie dough. "So, in the meantime, why don't we make another batch of cookies? But this time, we'll turn off the TV and remember to set the timer."

That made her laugh. "Let's stay right here to make sure these don't burn."

"And we can start a new tradition."

She shot a glance at the mistletoe.

"I said a new one." With a grin, he opened a cabinet and pulled out a bag of mini marshmallows. "Christmas hot cocoa."

"Okay." She would never say no to chocolate. "But what's the difference between regular hot chocolate and Christmas hot cocoa?"

He tapped the tip of her nose. "Your frame of mind."

12

Michael woke, more rested than he'd been in weeks. Not even eating too many of the delicious German Christmas cookies—he kept forgetting the actual name, so he called them that—last night had interfered with his sleep. That was all because of Sheridan.

As he remembered drinking hot cocoa and making sure the pan didn't burn, warmth flowed through him. He hadn't been looking for romance, but somehow it had found him.

Them.

But he didn't want to think beyond Christmas, even though she wasn't leaving until the thirty-first. Yes, whatever this was between them had an end date, but that might be why he wanted to make the most of the time they had together and not overanalyze anything.

A few emails were in his inbox. There was also a copy of the donation pledges that would be sent to the two rescues today. His team worked fast, but he was paying them to take care of stuff. This was extra, but it would be worth the expense.

Would the money change things with Sheridan?

Michael hoped not, but he would never know. She would be in Berry Lake or somewhere else when the money arrived, but he bet she would be excited if she found out. Not because she wanted something from him, but because he could travel and help others. When he was ready to settle down, he wanted to meet a woman like her.

He showered, dressed, and headed into the kitchen. The coffee pot was full, and empty grocery bags covered the table. Sheridan had set out the items they'd bought to make the ornaments. But one thing was missing.

With his cup in hand, he made his way to Hope's studio.

Sheridan sat cross-legged on the floor, giving him a great profile shot of her. A laptop was in front of her, a pencil rested between her lips, and a notepad lay to her right. She held a measuring tape across the width of a small seascape.

The sun shining through the French doors cast a glow around her. The halo effect was stunning. It also suited her. She'd become his personal Christmas angel.

He watched her until she placed the tape

measure on the floor. "Hard at work already?"

"I'm almost finished."

"Keep going." He didn't want to disturb her. A glance out the window showed blue skies. He needed to get outside and enjoy the beautiful weather. "I'm going to eat breakfast and then take a walk on the beach before we work on the ornaments. It's a gorgeous day outside."

"I'd love to join you."

Anticipation surged. "I was hoping you might. I'll let you know when."

A bowl of instant oatmeal and two cups of coffee later, Michael returned to the studio. "Is this a good time for you to take a break?"

Sheridan wiped her hands on her thighs. "Yes."

He eyed her black jeans and red sweater. "You look Christmassy."

"That was fully intentional." She studied his T-shirt. "Not to sound like your mom or sisters, but you might be cold without a jacket."

He laughed. "You sound just like them, so I'll tell you what I'd say to them. Men are always warm." Though she had a point. He'd been so excited to spend time with her, he hadn't considered the temperature outside. "I'll grab a sweater and meet you in the living room."

A few minutes later, they made their way down the wood walkway next to the cottage. A few wisps of clouds were overhead, but most of the sky was blue, making it seem more like summer than winter.

A slight breeze blew off the water, rustling through the beach grass and tossing the ends of Sheridan's hair.

"It's lovely out here." She headed to where the dry sand gave way to wet and lifted her face to the sun. "I can't imagine being anywhere else."

"Me, either." He couldn't stop staring at her. "Coastal Christmas for the win."

"That's for sure." She glanced in both directions. "Which way do you want to go?"

"Left." That seemed to be less crowded, and he fell into step beside her.

Waves rolled to shore, and a seabird flew overhead. The best part was having her at his side.

He laced his fingers with hers. "This okay?"

As she nodded, she squeezed his hand. "This is nice."

"It's relaxing."

"My mom has always told me everything works out for a reason, but I didn't believe her. She might be right."

"Sometimes, it takes time to see why something happens."

Sheridan stared at him. "Do you agree with my mom?"

Michael rubbed his beard and thought for a moment about buying a lottery ticket, staying at Von's beach house, and meeting Sheridan. None of those things would have happened if he had still been working.

"I do." He couldn't fully explain why, but he wanted to share something. "If I hadn't lost my job, I wouldn't have grown this beard and met you."

"The beard looks great, so it would be a shame if you didn't have it."

Her playful tone pleased him. He wanted nothing more than for her to be happy. "Good to know."

"If I were working at the gallery, I wouldn't have come to Indigo Bay."

It was his turn to squeeze her hand. She wouldn't just get over what happened, but Michael hoped he was helping her in some way. "I wish your dad hadn't done what he did, but I'm so glad you're here."

"So am I." She half laughed. "I'm amazed to say that. But it's true."

A lightness in his chest made him stand taller. He wanted to make sure she continued feeling that way.

A bird landed on the sand in front of them. Sheridan's face brightened. She grabbed her phone out of her pocket and took a picture. "I want to send this to my mom."

He snapped a photo of Sheridan so he would remember this walk.

And her.

* * *

Back at the house, he turned on the Christmas music channel before sitting next to Sheridan at the kitchen table. The way she'd organized everything brought a smile to his face. "This setup would make my mom and Marley proud."

She handed him a glass ornament they'd found on sale at the drugstore. They would each do three—one for Von, one for Hope, and one for themselves. "What about Madison?"

"She'd say it was too neat. She's not into lists or being organized, but she would create a masterpiece." He lowered his voice even though they were alone. "Between you and me, her ornaments are always the best ones."

"Your secret is safe with me."

If only he could tell her his. Instead, he removed the top of his ornament. "Any rules for decorating?"

"Be creative. But that's not really a rule, only a suggestion."

"Good, then I can get messy."

"Go ahead, but you're cleaning it up."

"For an only child, you have the big-sister tone down."

"I use it for babysitting, but it seems to work well on you, too."

He placed his hands over his chest and feigned an injury. "You wound me."

Humor gleamed in her eyes. "You'll survive."

"Maybe with a few more of those cookies we made."

Ignoring him, she squeezed red acrylic paint inside her ornament and then swirled it to extend the stripe all the way around. She did the same thing with white.

"Yours looks like a candy cane." Michael picked up the green bottle. "I'm going for a green and red effect."

He spun the first bit and then added more until satisfied. The red came next. By the time he finished, all the glass was covered.

Sheridan leaned closer. "That's pretty. It'll look beautiful with the red ribbon."

He placed the ornament upside down in a disposable cup to dry. "I forgot about the ribbon."

"These are coming out better than I expected. And they're easier to do than decoupage with tissue paper. That would be a big mess."

"Is that something you do when you babysit?"

She nodded. "It was weird babysitting again after not doing it for so many years. I don't know what kids are used to these days, but I wasn't about to let them watch TV or play video games since I was being paid to take care of them. So we did crafts, played games, went outside. The parents loved it."

"What about the kids?"

"They put up a fight until they realized I wouldn't relent."

He made another ornament with white, red, and green. "I wonder what life will be like for my nephew."

"Monroe, right?"

Flutters filled Michael's stomach. "Yes. His childhood will be different from mine."

"Depends on how much their parents limit his screen time. Whether they have their own tablet, computer, or phone."

"You've thought about this for someone who doesn't have kids." Unless she wanted them sooner rather than later. He tugged at his collar.

"Not really." She poured green paint into an ornament. "Some women came into the cupcake shop last week and were discussing it. I think they all had kids. But my friend Missy and I ended up talking about it. She has no kids, either. So I'm not sure why we did that."

He left kid discussions to his married siblings. "You not only make cookies but cupcakes?"

"I didn't bake the cupcakes, but I frosted some. I only fill in when people call out. But the paycheck was nice."

"How is this one?" He held up his ornament, wanting to take her thoughts off what happened in Berry Lake. He wanted to turn Indigo Bay into a bubble world for Sheridan, where nothing from her past would ruin Christmas.

"Oh, I like how the three colors turned out."

"Yours are better."

She shimmied her shoulders. "Thank you."

"So, I've been thinking."

"Should I be nervous?"

"Haha." He added yellow to an ornament. Time to go all-in with the colors on this last one. "You mentioned attending the tree lighting on Christmas Eve."

She nodded. "I texted Hope about it. She said we should get in line around three. The mayor turns on the lights at five."

"The day's wide open for me."

"Me, too."

"So, after the lighting, how about we come back here and have lasagna for dinner?"

Her lips formed a perfect O. "You remembered my family's tradition."

He nodded. "But lasagna is also easy if we buy a frozen one. We can also get bread. I'm not sure what else you have with it."

"Green beans, salad, and wine."

"Works for me."

She shifted positions in her chair. "I've never made prime rib, but if you want it for Christmas dinner, I could try."

His face heated. "Uh..."

Her gaze narrowed. "What?"

"I already made plans."

"With your Patterson relatives?"

She had it all wrong. Michael would fix that.

"No. For us. Reservations, actually. It was going to be a surprise."

"Sorry." Her eyes twinkled. "Except I'm not sorry. I'm excited. Thank you for doing that."

"It'll be a different Christmas for both of us, but I thought eating out would be nice. And this is on me, okay?"

She hesitated.

Her expression told him she wanted to say no, but he wanted to do this for her. "Please?"

"Okay, but I'm buying Christmas Eve dinner."

That was easier than he imagined it would be. "Deal."

As she swirled an ornament, her gaze met his. "This Christmas had the possibility of being one of the worst. But thanks to you, it's turning into one of the best. Thank you for that."

He straightened. "You're welcome. And Christmas is still two days away. We have a lot more celebrating to do."

13

O n the morning of December twenty-fourth, Sheridan stood on the deck, watching the waves roll to shore. Clouds had moved in, but the sky wasn't completely covered. She'd assumed her Christmas would be blue, not merry. She'd never been so happy to be wrong.

A door opened and closed.

Michael stood behind Sheridan and wrapped his arms around her stomach. "The ornaments aren't dry."

She leaned against him, soaking up his warmth. "They'll be ready when Hope and Von return."

When it's time for me to leave.

Her chest tightened, imagining herself saying goodbye to Michael. She gripped the deck's railing until her knuckles went white.

"Hey, are you okay?" he asked. "You're all tense."

Oh, no. Sheridan didn't want to ruin the time they had left together by worrying about the future. She would concentrate on today and tomorrow. Everything else could wait.

She let go of the rail. "I'm fine."

"So am I." He nuzzled against her neck. His breath was warm against her skin. "Do we have what we need for the next two days, or should we make another run to the market?"

She laughed. "More than enough. I can't believe you bought eggnog."

"Someone left a coupon by it." With his hands on her shoulders, he turned Sheridan so she faced him. "I didn't want to forget anything that might be a Christmas tradition."

Will he forget me while he travels the world?

Her breath hitched.

Nope. She wasn't going there. Instead, she kissed his cheek, above where his beard started. "Thank you."

His mouth slanted into a wry grin. "You're welcome, but I'm doing this for me, too."

"I'm amazed it's Christmas Eve." And that she was in his arms with the mistletoe only a few feet away.

"What time do we need to head to Main Street?"

"Three o'clock. What do you want to do until then?"

Mischief lit his eyes. "I have a few ideas—going on a walk, kissing, watching another movie, kissing."

Her phone rang.

"Or answering the phone," he added. "Then kissing."

The ringtone made her stomach knot. She bit her lip.

"Sheridan?" Concern filled Michael's voice.

"It's... Sal." She'd almost said her father, but he'd lost that title in November.

"Don't answer."

A million thoughts ran through her mind, but one came to the forefront. "What if something's wrong?"

Michael lowered his arms to his sides, and she missed the warmth of his touch. "I'll go inside to give you privacy."

The phone rang again.

"Stay." Her voice cracked. "Please."

He touched her shoulder. "I'm right here."

With a nod, she raised the phone to her ear. "Hello."

"Things with Remy aren't working out." Sal sounded impatient. "I need you at the gallery, Sheri-doll."

His use of her pet name melted Sheridan's

heart. He hadn't called her that since Deena entered the picture. Unexpected hope blossomed. Maybe Sheridan would get her dad back.

She clutched the phone, torn between wanting to tell him she'd be there as soon as possible and needing him to own up to how badly he hurt her.

"You've got this, beautiful," Michael said.

And she did, but hearing him was a wonderful reminder. This phone call was more than she expected, and though she was hopeful, it wasn't enough. "Is that all you have to say to me?"

"What more do you need?"

She stared at Michael, drawing extra strength from him. She took a breath and another. "You gave my job and apartment to someone else. I need to hear more than I'm needed at the gallery. I need an apology for what you did."

Sal mumbled something. "Deena said you'd be difficult about this."

It always came back to his new wife. And though Sheridan was clinging to a sliver of hope, she wouldn't be a doormat. "Then ask her to help you out."

Silence filled the line.

"Look, I shouldn't have listened to Deena. Things with Remy have been"—he lowered his voice as if he didn't want anyone else to hear—"a disaster. She misunderstood how our commission worked and had a flash sale while I was away. Every piece was discounted fifty percent."

Ouch. Sheridan cringed. Artists earned anywhere from forty to seventy percent of the sales price, depending on the contract. The gallery would have to make up the money. "That's going to hurt."

"If you had trained her—"

"Don't blame me for this."

"Okay, fine." He sighed. "I'm sorry. I made a mistake letting you go. Do you want me to beg?"

It wasn't the best apology, but she wasn't like Michael, who had more family members than he could count on two hands. Sheridan had her parents, and she wanted them in her life. She needed both despite what had happened at Thanksgiving. "You don't have to beg."

"Can you be here by lunchtime?" he asked without missing a beat.

"No. I'm in South Carolina. I return on the thirty-first."

"That's too far away. I need you here before that."

Again, she wanted to tell him yes, but she hesitated. As much as she wanted a dad, she needed him to want her in return. "If I change my flight, there's a fee. I can't afford to pay that."

"I'll pay for it. Try to be at the gallery when it opens on the twenty-sixth, so we can end the year strong."

"I can't work miracles."

"No, but you can turn things around."

His confidence in her abilities sent pride rushing through her. She reached out to Michael with her free hand. "I'll try."

"Please, Sheridan. This is important. I know I hurt you, but I'll make it up to you." He sounded contrite. "I promise."

He'd broken his promises before, but she wanted to believe he had learned his lesson. "So, Remy…?"

"No longer works here."

"What about Owen?"

"He's doing stuff behind the scenes. I don't know if it's making a difference yet, but we can discuss that when you're here."

He was saying all the right things, but Sheridan had to ask about one more person. "And Deena?"

"She told me she wouldn't interfere in the gallery again."

Okay, that was progress. Sheridan didn't want to leave Indigo Bay early, but this was her career—her future—and her family at stake. She had no other choice. Michael would understand. "I'll call the airline about changing my flight."

"Thank you." Her father's relief was palpable. "I knew you'd come through for me."

He still believed in her. She wiggled her toes.

"Text me the info and your confirmation number, so I can pay the change fee," he added.

"I will."

"Call them now. If you arrive today, we can spend tonight together."

Her heart nearly exploded. He remembered Christmas Eve was his holiday this year. He hadn't forgotten about her. She mattered to him. He still loved her. "I'll do what I can."

"Try your best. See you soon, Sheri-doll." With that, he hung up.

As she stared at the phone, a mix of emotions ran through her.

"You okay?"

She smiled. "I am."

Michael hugged her. "Good job standing up to your father."

"I'm happy I did. He apologized and admitted he had made a mistake." She blew out a breath. "I never thought that would happen."

"So, why did he call?"

"He's having issues at the gallery. He needs me to turn things around for him."

Michael studied her. "What about your stepmother and her kids?"

"Remy no longer works at the gallery. My dad said his wife won't interfere again."

A smile spread across Michael's face. He hugged her. "That's wonderful."

"I almost can't believe it." She leaned into Michael and held on tight. The scent of him tickled her nose, and she wished he would go to Berry Lake with her. Too bad her hometown would be the definition of boring to someone who wanted to travel the world. "I never expected my father to call me or want me to come back."

"How do you feel?"

"I'm so happy, but at the same time, I'm in shock."

"Take your time to process everything. You don't have to rush home."

"He needs me there right away."

Michael let go of her, but he kept his hands on her shoulders. "What do you need?"

You.

The realization almost made her laugh. She was being ridiculous. They barely knew each other. A few kisses and holiday traditions didn't make a relationship. Not that they'd taken the time to put a name on what they were doing. Whatever they had was temporary. Whether she left today, tomorrow, or on the thirty-first, the result would be the same—they wouldn't be together. That simplified everything, even if her heart disagreed.

She raised her chin. "I need my job at the gallery."

His Adam's apple bobbed. "I'm happy for you."

"But?"

Concern clouded his eyes. "After what you told

me about your father, I'm not convinced changing your plans to suit him is for the best. Yes, he apologized, but it's easy for him to tell you how much things have changed when you're not there."

"But he's my dad. He's learned his lesson."

A vein pulsed at his jaw. "What if he hasn't?"

She understood Michael was trying to protect her. He probably did this with his sisters and friends, but he didn't understand her situation. He couldn't.

"I won't see the worst in him." The words rushed out. "I can't do that. I need things—him—to have changed."

"I'm sorry if I upset you, but I'm worried about you, and I'm not sure you can trust him."

"It's okay, but he's my father. This will work out."

It must.

He caressed her cheek. "I hope so, for your sake."

Now came the hard part. A lump formed in her throat. "The only problem is he needs me at the gallery on the twenty-sixth."

Michael's jaw dropped. "You'll have to leave today or tomorrow."

She nodded. "I want to stay until the thirty-first."

"I want you to stay until then, too."

"If I could…"

"But you need to go home."

"I do. This is my chance to prove myself with the gallery."

"You don't have to prove anything to your father or anyone else."

She stared at the deck. Michael was correct. "No, but I want to go home. If you want to come or visit—"

"You could stay here instead."

"I can't." What she wanted—needed—clashed with what he wanted. "My dad's gallery means everything to me. It's my job, my passion, my life. My dad is far from perfect, but he's giving me the chance to work there again. I need to do more than couch-surfing at friends' houses and bumming around."

As Michael's face fell, he stepped away from her. "Wow. I didn't realize that's how you see me."

"It's not. I meant we're at different places."

"That's interesting, because you agreed we were in the same spot."

Heat flooded her face. "I care about you."

"You have a funny way of showing it." His shoulders sagged. "I thought you saw me differently, but you're like everybody else who sees me as nothing more than a kid who never grew up. A loser."

"I never said that."

"You didn't have to." He moved toward the

French doors. "You should call the airlines so you can change your flight. You might luck out and be able to find one for today."

"But what about our plans? The community tree and lasagna for dinner."

"You could be on an airplane by then."

"I'm sorry." The words sounded weak to her ears. "If I had a choice—"

"There's always a choice," he cut her off. "I hope you don't regret yours. I'll get out of your way so you can arrange your flight and pack. If there's anything you didn't finish for Hope, leave a list on the counter."

Sheridan had only known him a few days, so her heart shouldn't be breaking, but it was. "That's all you have to say?"

"Have a safe trip home." He opened the French door. "Goodbye."

15

Goodbye.

The word echoed through Michael as if someone had rung a giant gong. He grabbed his jacket, his car keys, and one of the ornaments they'd purchased at the fair. His feet carried him to the front door. As his hand touched the knob, he hesitated.

Emotions were high. He and Sheridan should talk because he had doubts about what would happen with her father—no one changed overnight. But she didn't want to hear that. Besides, he wouldn't forget what she'd said.

I need to do more than couch-surfing at friends' houses and bumming around.

The words had punched his gut then and now, making him relive his family's stupid intervention, their concerns over his job situation, and the many comments about Mikey never growing up.

In case anyone failed to notice, he was an adult who had his teeth cleaned every six months, paid his bills, and filed his taxes on time.

He opened the door, stepped out, and then slammed it shut, not caring that the wreath rattled as did the Christmas lights.

Everyone was wrong about him, including Sheridan.

For a second, he'd been tempted to tell her about winning the lottery, but he shouldn't have to. No one needed to prove themselves to anyone else. Besides, winning had been nothing except him being lucky. It was what he had done since winning that showed he was mature and responsible.

Yes, knowing he would be in a completely different place in life in a couple of weeks would have changed her opinion about him. But he didn't want to be with someone like that. Her father might need Sheridan, but Michael didn't.

And if he kept telling himself that, he might come to believe it.

The wind blew. He reached up to adjust his cap and realized he wasn't wearing it. The beach house was behind him, but he kept moving forward. When he reached Main Street, he slipped into the first souvenir shop he saw. The stack of Santa hats caught his eye, but he grabbed a beanie instead.

Celebrating Christmas left a sour taste in his mouth, but he wanted to hang the ornament with the name of the animal rescue on it—free publicity for them.

He wandered along Main Street, unsure where he was going, but knowing he didn't want to be at the beach house. He might spend tonight at his parents' place, and then he could return to Indigo Bay after Sheridan left. That sounded like a plan.

People were getting in line, so he stood behind a couple.

"Come on, Lizzy." The guy, who had a military haircut, put his arm around a pretty brunette. "Tell me what you're wishing for?"

"You ask every year, and the answer is always the same."

He kissed her. "You might change your mind."

"And risk my wish not coming true." She shook her head. "Give it up, Mitch, and go buy me a hot chocolate from Sweet Caroline's."

"Your wish is my command, but remember what Caroline told us about Christmas wishes being the most powerful wish of all."

She turned slightly, patting her pregnant stomach. "This little guy is proof that's true."

"Don't forget. I wished for him, too." The man kissed her forehead. "I'll be right back. Text me if you need anything else."

Michael turned away from the happy couple. Their sugary sweetness didn't disgust him. No, a different emotion welled inside him—envy. He wanted someone to be at his side when he made a wish. He wanted...

No, not Sheridan.

Still, thinking about her made his heart ache.

He would get over it.

Get over her.

As the minutes passed, the temperature dropped. Darker clouds appeared overhead. People around him wondered aloud if it would rain.

Mitch returned with three hot chocolates. He held a cup up to Michael. "Want one?"

"Please." Michael took it. "Thanks."

"Merry Christmas." The guy turned to his wife.

A woman wearing a Santa hat and a safety vest walked along the line. "We'll be opening for wishes and ornament hanging in a few minutes. Groups will go up to the tree one at a time. The line will go faster if you know your wish."

Michael didn't need to make a wish. In a few short weeks, he would be able to buy whatever he wanted.

What about Sheridan?

The question was so clear, as if someone had spoken it. He glanced around, but no one was paying attention to him. He was also the only person who appeared to be alone.

But he didn't need to wish for Sheridan. Sure, he would have enjoyed spending Christmas with her. They would've had fun, celebrating and experiencing their various family traditions. Someday, he would meet a woman like her—only someone who didn't see him as a couch-surfing loser.

Okay, that was what he was right now.

He had a bed to sleep in thanks to his future brother-in-law. But this lifestyle was his choice. Not that Sheridan knew that.

Never mind.

He should wish for someone special in his life to spend Christmas with. Not this year—there was no time for that to happen—but next year. Then, he wouldn't have to keep secrets from his family. Everyone would be together, too. If he had someone with him, he would no longer be the odd person out.

"You're next," the woman who'd made the announcement earlier said. "Make a wish and then hang your ornament."

Michael tossed his empty cocoa cup in the garbage can and then stepped forward. The tree had to be at least forty feet tall. Most ornaments hung on the bottom where people could reach. He closed his eyes.

I wish I could spend Christmas with someone special. Not this year. But next year and every year after that.

He went to hang the ornament but froze before the ribbon touched the branch.

There was a more important wish he wanted to make.

Michael closed his eyes again.

I wish for Sheridan to get the Christmas of her dreams, one where she's surrounded by the people who love her.

Satisfied, he hung the ornament. The bulb bounced slightly before settling. He stepped away.

Idiot.

He'd wasted a Christmas wish.

No biggie. The lottery money would make all his wishes come true. Even if he never met someone special, he would be fine.

Von believed the wishes made on this tree often came true, which was what drew the crowds to Indigo Bay. Maybe Michael would return next Christmas Eve and make a wish for himself. But the only place he wanted to be right now was anywhere but here.

He glanced at the line and saw Sheridan toward the back. She mustn't have been able to get a flight out this afternoon.

Wonder what she will wish for.

None of his business.

While she waited to hang her ornament, he would return to the beach house and pack his things. He would spend a couple of days at his parents' house and then go back to Indigo Bay on the twenty-sixth when he knew Sheridan would be gone.

The thought of being alone sucked, but this was for the best.

* * *

Sheridan stood in line with what appeared to be all of Indigo Bay to hang her ornament on the community Christmas tree. She was near the end. It was her fault for taking too much time with the airline to reschedule her flight for tomorrow morning and then dawdling in the empty, silent beach house. She'd also texted a link to her father where he could pay the change fee.

She rechecked her phone. No reply. He must be busy.

A breeze blew, sending a chill through her. She zipped her jacket all the way to her chin. Not that the cooler temperature appeared to bother anyone. Children giggled, some people sang Christmas carols, and a yellow lab barked.

She'd glimpsed Michael near the front of the line, but she never found him again.

A young woman wearing a Santa hat, an orange safety vest, and a smile moved alongside the line. "Things are moving quickly. You'll go up to the tree with your party. The line will move faster if you know your wish ahead of time."

What do I want to wish for?

Her dad had called, when only yesterday,

hearing from him had seemed like an impossible dream. Part of her wanted to wish for her and Michael to spend Christmas together.

As if on cue, Sheridan saw him. She didn't recognize the beanie he wore, but it was him. "Michael."

He stopped, but he didn't glance her way.

Her heart sank, but she had to try again. "Please."

He came toward her, but he said nothing.

"I don't fly out until the morning. All I have to do is hang my ornament, and then we can spend Christmas Eve together."

"No."

The air rushed out of her lungs. "But we planned it all out."

"That was before you decided to leave."

"I'd be leaving on the thirty-first, anyway."

He shrugged.

"I have to go. This is my work. My life. My family."

"I hope it works out the way you want." He shoved his fingertips into his pockets. "Merry Christmas."

He walked away. Sheridan was tempted to call his name again, but they could talk at the beach house. She would apologize for what she had said about him, and everything would be okay.

A half hour later, she reached the front of the line.

Another woman in a Santa hat and safety vest motioned her forward. "It's your turn."

At the tree, Sheridan held out the ornament and closed her eyes.

I wish I could spend Christmas with Michael.

She hung her ornament on the tree and stepped away. The lighting was at five. They'd planned on watching together, but she wanted to see Michael now, so she headed to the cottage.

His SUV wasn't parked in the driveway. Okay, no need to let the dread in her stomach grow. He might have gone to the market if he realized he'd forgotten something. Except, she'd told him they needed nothing.

With shaky fingers, she unlocked the door and opened it. "Michael."

No answer. The house was as quiet as when she'd left.

The door to his room was open. His duffel bag was gone.

Gone.

The word reverberated through her.

She plopped onto the mattress.

A weight pressed on the center of her chest.

He hadn't given her a chance to apologize or explain or make things better.

He'd left.

Her breath hitched. She struggled to fill her lungs with oxygen.

What was happening? Why did she miss him already?

Sheridan headed to the living room. The Christmas tree reminded her of Michael so much, it might as well have been screaming his name. She adjusted an ornament.

Silence surrounded her, and she hated it.

You wanted to be alone for Christmas.

That was why she'd come to Indigo Bay.

Except that wasn't what Sheridan wanted now. She wanted to spend Christmas Eve with Michael, doing all the things they'd planned. Only he no longer wanted that.

Because of her and what she'd said.

Do something.

She had to do something, but what?

Her mom might know. She hit her mom's contact info. The phone rang. Once, twice…

"Hello, sweetheart."

Her mom's warm greeting was just what Sheridan needed. "I'll be flying in tomorrow. I should be home for Christmas dinner."

"Did something happen in Indigo Bay?"

Yes, but that wasn't the reason she was returning early. "Dad called. He needs me at the gallery on the twenty-sixth. Remy didn't work out."

"What about your roommate?"

"He left."

"Oh, I thought the two of you were getting closer."

So did she. "We had fun together."

"Do you need a ride from the airport?"

"No. Not on Christmas." Sheridan wondered if her dad might want to pick her up. She would ask when he replied about paying the change fee. If not, she would take a shuttle or a bus. "Enjoy it with Max and his daughters. I'll be there as soon as I can."

"I don't mind." Her mom didn't hesitate to reply, which was typical for the woman who had made multitasking an art form.

It would be so easy to say yes, but her mother needed to see to the animals and cook dinner. She deserved a day off from the other things. "I do."

"Okay." The word came out slowly as if her mom wasn't convinced.

Sheridan didn't want her mom to second-guess. "It really is okay."

"Are you sure you want to return to the gallery?"

Whoa. Sheridan hadn't expected that question. The answer sat on the tip of her tongue. She imagined Michael, but that was over. "It's all I want, Mom."

"I doubt anything has changed since you left."

Sheridan gripped the phone. "You mean Deena."

"Yes." Her mom sounded exasperated. "She's as boastful and annoying as ever."

"I asked Dad about her. He told me Deena's finished interfering with the gallery."

"Well, that's a relief." Sarcasm poured from each word. "If it's true."

Sheridan understood her mom's reaction, but... "Dad wouldn't have called me if he wasn't serious about wanting me back."

"You're right."

At least Sheridan wasn't the only one who thought so. "I just wish Michael hadn't left, so we could spend Christmas Eve together."

A beat passed. "It sounds like he was more than a roommate."

Sheridan weighed her words. "I liked him."

"Past tense?"

She couldn't tell whether her mom was curious or worried. "Yes."

Silence filled the line.

"Well," her mom said finally. "Your grandma claimed Yuletide magic made anything better."

Sheridan almost smiled thinking about her grandmother talking about Yuletide and the importance of picking out the right yule log. Those magical tales had fueled childhood fantasies of stepping inside a painting or storybook.

She swallowed a sigh. "I hope so, because I already miss Michael."

"You didn't know him long, though." Her *mom* tone was coming out. At least she wasn't going all Mama Bear yet.

"No, I didn't." But that didn't matter to Sheridan's heart. At least it still beat. That had to count for something. "Maybe between Grandma's Yuletide magic and the wish I made on the town's Christmas tree, everything will turn out okay."

"It will." The words rushed out. "You want to know how I know this?"

"Yes, please."

"Things were looking more dire than usual with the rescue. But then, we received an anonymous pledge for twenty-five thousand dollars." The relief in her mom's voice was palpable.

"That's wonderful."

"It'll cover our overdue vet bills and let us start a medical fund for future needs."

"I'm so happy for you. Guess someone needed an end-of-the-year tax deduction."

"That's just it. The money won't arrive until mid-January. Not that I care when we get it. That much will make a difference anytime." Her mom sighed. "I only wish we knew who the donor is, but some people don't want the recognition, and I respect that."

"It's still a Christmas blessing."

"Yes. And there is at least one waiting for you. So don't stop hoping."

Sheridan nearly laughed. Hope was all she had left. "Thanks."

"I can't wait to see you."

"I'm looking forward to it, too." Sheridan tried to sound cheerful, but she wasn't sure she succeeded. "Merry Christmas, Mom."

15

Merry Christmas to me.

The house was so quiet, so empty.

Michael had wanted to be alone for the holidays, but now, the silence grated on him.

He stared at his parents' tree. Each ornament held a story, but today that brought no laughter.

No joy.

The multicolor lights blinked. On and off. On and off. He preferred white bulbs.

No presents sat under the branches. The stockings didn't overflow with gifts. He missed the scent of cinnamon rolls baking in the oven. He'd forgotten to share that tradition with Sheridan.

I don't fly out until the morning. All I have to do is hang my ornament, and then we can spend Christmas Eve together.

He should have said yes.

Y-E-S.

Instead of saying that, he'd packed his bag and left the beach house before she returned. Why hadn't he given her last night?

Michael made himself a cup of coffee. He took a sip when his phone rang—his mom.

Time to put on his game face. "Hey, Mom. Merry Christmas."

"Merry Christmas to you. How are you?"

"Good. I'm at your house."

"Did something happen?"

"My roommate had to fly home, so I came here." Sheridan was probably at the airport waiting to depart. "I'll go to Von's place tomorrow."

By then, all traces of her will have disappeared.

"Well, the kids want to open gifts, but I wanted to check in first." His mom sounded like she was smiling. "Enjoy your quiet Christmas."

"Have fun at your chaotic one."

"Honey, you sound sad." The way his mom picked up on their emotions was her superpower. "It's difficult to lose a girlfriend and then a new friend, but you're young, and you'll meet other women."

Except he might not ever meet another woman like Sheridan.

Was she perfect? No, but she had seemed perfect for him.

"Thanks, Mom." He forced the words from his dry throat. "Tell Dad merry Christmas from me."

"I love you, Mikey."

"Love you."

As he hung up, thoughts of Sheridan overloaded his brain. Everything had been going well. She had no idea about the money he'd won. He'd thought she accepted him being unemployed without a place to live, but nothing she said was untrue. He was couch-surfing and had been for a couple of months. Yesterday, he'd been staying in his future brother-in-law's bedroom, a step up from sleeping in a friend's living room.

But she'd hurt him.

And he'd shut down.

The way he always did. Scratch that, the way Mikey, youngest in the family, had since he'd been old enough to react.

Except he didn't want to be Mikey any longer, which meant it was time to change.

She'd invited him to Berry Lake, which suggested she didn't hate the person he was, but he hadn't given her the courtesy of an answer. He'd asked her to stay.

He'd been selfish. Her dream was her dad's gallery.

Michael should have said yes, continued working online and over the phone with his team. Someone else would turn in the ticket, but if he needed to be local that day, he could fly here.

Is it too late?

She would be at the airport this morning. All he had to do was find her.

He tossed his toiletries into his duffel bag, which still contained his laptop and clothes, and then swung the strap over his shoulder. He had his keys, his phone, and a jacket. That should do it.

The drive took forever. Worry knotted his muscles.

What if her flight had taken off?

Adrenaline surged through him. He gripped the steering wheel.

Not wanting to miss seeing her, Michael pulled into the valet parking area, grabbed his bag off the front seat, and spoke to the attendant quickly. His conversation with Sheridan might be over in a few minutes. Still, he hoped she wanted him to go to Berry Lake with her.

Being together was the most important thing. Indigo Bay or Charleston or Berry Lake—as long as he was with her, the location meant nothing.

It was time to say goodbye to everyone's annoying little brother, Mikey, who kept messing up, and become Michael, an adult who didn't react to every little thing. Michael wouldn't sulk when his feelings were hurt, or he didn't get his way. He wouldn't turn down an invitation out of spite. Instead, he would offer to make this the best

Christmas he could for Sheridan.

Michael prayed she didn't turn him down the way he had her.

* * *

Sheridan hadn't expected the airport to be so busy on Christmas morning. She rolled her suitcase away from the self-check-in kiosk, trying to keep her breathing calm and the tears at bay. As soon as she put enough distance between herself and the other passengers in line, she phoned her dad.

One ring, two rings, three rings.

"This better be important." His voice was growly. "It's still dark here."

Okay, she'd woken him. That explained why he sounded like that. "I'm at the airport. The change fee hasn't been paid."

Silence filled the line.

She gripped her cell phone. "Dad?"

"There's been a change of plans."

Sheridan's throat closed. She swallowed. "What kind of change?"

"Remy apologized. She wants her job back."

"Wait. I thought you fired her."

"No, she quit after I yelled at her. Anyway, I don't need you at the gallery."

This wasn't happening. Not again. "But Remy has no idea what she's doing."

"That's your fault for not training her."

"You said you were struggling."

"Owen offered to help me."

Sheridan wanted to remind him that her stepbrother had no art or sales experience, but she pressed her lips together instead.

"That's why I didn't pay the change fee," he continued. "Stay where you are. You're not needed here."

A lump, hotter than a charcoal briquet at a summer barbeque, burned in her throat. "I'm at the airport and turned in my rental car."

"You can fly home, but I'm not paying the change fee. Ask your mother to cover it."

Sheridan went numb. Michael had been right. Nothing had changed. Misguided hope had turned her father's call into a dream come to life. But it hadn't been real. His new family still meant more to him than her.

But she had to ask one thing. "Did Deena tell Remy to return to the gallery?"

"After I told Deena you would take over again, she made me realize I overreacted. She offered to help Remy figure things out."

Of course, Deena had. And she would do whatever she could to keep Sheridan out of her father's life and the gallery.

"Everything will be fine," he said in a matter-of-fact tone.

"I hope so, but not for you or Deena or her horrible spawn, but because Berry Lake needs a gallery for artists like Hope Ryan. They need to show their works locally, and tourists need a place to buy something more substantial than a trinket from the souvenir store. So, please don't screw this up or let Deena get her hands on your gallery because she'll dump the place at the first sign of trouble."

"Sheridan—"

"You might not see the truth, but I do. Finally. You've chosen Deena and her kids over me for the last time. I'm blocking your number. I put my heart and soul into the gallery, but I'm done. If it goes under, that's on you. I refuse to let you dash my hopes again."

Silence filled the line.

"Goodbye, Sal. I wish you luck. Because you're going to need it."

Sheridan waited for a response, but she heard nothing. The line had disconnected.

The numbness continued to grip her. A good thing, or she'd be crying her eyes out at the airport.

Her hand remained steady as she blocked Sal's number.

It's over.

It was really over.

She'd lost her father and the gallery. But worst of all, she'd lost Michael. She'd been so desperate to regain the first two, she'd lashed out at him.

Sheridan didn't care that it was super early in Berry Lake. She hit the number for her mom's landline. If anyone were up at this hour, they would be in the kitchen to answer.

"Hello."

It was one of Max's daughters, but she hadn't talked to her enough on the phone to recognize the voice. "Is Sabine there? It's Sheridan."

"Merry Christmas. Everyone is still asleep. They went to midnight Mass, so they were up late. My dad texted me when they got home. I just got off my shift and came over here. I can wake her."

Nell, who worked in the emergency department at the local hospital, was on the phone.

"No. Let her sleep." Sheridan's voice cracked.

"Are you okay?"

"I'm at the airport."

"We're so excited to see you."

"My dad didn't pay the change fee." She blinked, but that didn't stop the tears from welling in her eyes. "He changed his mind about having me work at the gallery again. He told me to stay here because he doesn't need me. And I don't have enough money to cover the change fee. I turned in my rental car, even though my mom and your dad prepaid for the entire time. Now I'm standing in the Charleston Airport on Christmas, and I have no idea what to do."

Sheridan wiped the wetness from her eyes.

"Hey. It's going to be okay." Noises sounded in the background. "I'm getting my credit card. I'll pay your change fee."

"Thank you, Nell." More tears fell. "This means so…"

A male hand holding a credit card appeared in front of her. She followed the arm up to see…

Michael.

"Put the fee on this." His serious tone matched the look in his eyes. "It'll be easier to do it this way than over the phone."

"Sheridan? Are you still there?" Nell asked.

"I'm here." Sheridan sniffled. "I need to get off. The fee is covered."

"Do you need us to pick you up?"

Hearing Nell say *us* warmed Sheridan's heart. "I'll text you."

"We'll be waiting to hear from you. And I'm sorry your father did that."

"Thanks." Michael continued to stare at her. "I'll talk to you soon."

"When Sabine wakes up, I'll tell her what happened. Bye."

She disconnected from the call. "What are you doing here?"

"I want to apologize."

"I'm the one who needs to say I'm sorry."

"I was an idiot. I should have never left the way

I did. I ruined Christmas Eve."

"Everything you said about Sal was correct."

"I heard. I'm sorry." Michael put the credit card in her hand. "Use this to go home. And if the invitation still stands, I'd like to go with you. A white Christmas in Washington sounds good."

This was typical Michael, and she loved it. "No."

His eyes widened. "No?"

"We're not spending Christmas in Washington. We're celebrating in Indigo Bay, the way we planned."

"But your family…"

"Will understand. I don't want to go home. Yesterday, Sal's call filled me with hope thinking he loved me, and things had changed. But you were right. They hadn't. Logically, I knew this when I left Berry Lake, but my heart and the little girl inside me who was desperate for her father's love and approval hadn't figured it out yet, but now I know. And my biggest regret isn't giving Sal a second chance. It was losing you for a silly pipe dream and not being able to do anything to get you back."

"It wasn't silly, and I'm right here. I'm not going anyplace without you." He kissed her softly on the lips. "Let's go to Indigo Bay."

"I turned in my rental car."

"Then it's a good thing I have my SUV."

"The lasagna is in the freezer."

"That can be lunch. I forgot to cancel our dinner reservations." He held her hands. "It's time to celebrate."

"That whole wish-on-an-ornament tradition works."

He brushed his lips over hers. "Then we'll be here next Christmas Eve."

* * *

New Year's Eve

Between Christmas and New Year's Eve, Michael couldn't believe how close he and Sheridan had become. They hung out, watched TV, put together puzzles, cooked some food, and burned a few meals when they were distracted. He'd answered her questions about all his calls, but he hated not being able to tell her the truth. One conversation still bothered him.

You're getting a lot of interviews. Any job offers?

No. They aren't for jobs.

Then what? You've got a secret girlfriend.

That would be you. Except my family knows about you.

So the calls…

Business.

Like research?

Something like that.

She'd brought up his web meetings and calls a

few more times. He'd finally realized he had to let her in on his secret before it drove a wedge through their new relationship. He'd lost her once. He wouldn't lose her again.

His attorney thought telling her was a significant risk, especially since he wouldn't ask her to sign a non-disclosure agreement. But Michael had been adamant about no NDA. He trusted her with his heart and would trust her with this, too.

Except the timing had never been right.

She'd cancelled her return flight to remain in Indigo Bay. But as of today, December thirty-first, they were no longer alone.

The extended Patterson clan, who wanted to make up for all the missed holiday gatherings with this one, had invaded their quiet sanctuary.

Hope and Von's house was not only crowded but also loud, with music playing over the many conversations. Food kept appearing, and the supply of drinks seemed never-ending. Adults mingled with kids. There were even three babies, including Monroe, who had grown while away. All were having a good time.

Michael never thought he'd love anyone more than his family.

That was, until he met Sheridan DeMarco.

He enjoyed introducing her to his family, but one thing stood between them—his winning lottery ticket. He needed to tell her. And he hoped—

prayed—nothing would change when she found out the truth.

Michael held her hand. "Let's go outside."

"It's almost midnight."

He laughed. "We'll hear the countdown from there."

As they stood on the deck, a breeze blew off the water. The crystal-clear night meant colder temperatures. Michael wrapped his arm around her to keep her warm. This was becoming a habit, one he enjoyed.

Sheridan leaned into him. "Tonight has been wonderful. Your family is nice, if a tad overwhelming. I'm glad I stayed."

"Everyone likes you. Dare I say, they like you better than me?"

"Sure they do, beloved baby of the family." She laughed. "But hearing that makes me happy because I like them."

He needed to tell her so much, but he wasn't sure where to start. It had to be tonight, though. New Year's Eve was the perfect time, so they could begin the new year with no secrets between them.

Voices inside counted down. "Ten, nine, eight, seven, six, five, four, three, two, one."

Horns blew, and people shouted.

"Happy New Year." Sheridan kissed him. "I hope it's not too soon, but I love you."

Fireworks exploded inside his heart. "I love you."

He pressed his lips against hers as a declaration of his love and wanting to be with her forever.

Her arms wrapped around him. Her fingers twirled the edges of his hair.

He needed to stop so he could tell her about the money.

Michael backed away from Sheridan, but he remained touching her. "Here's to a wonderful new year."

"Despite us being unemployed and homeless." She half laughed.

"We may be those things, but in a few days, we won't be penniless."

Her face pinched. "I don't understand."

He glanced through the window at his family, who continued to laugh, blow horns, drink champagne, and toss confetti. "They don't know yet. I want to tell you first."

"Tell me what?" Her gaze clouded. "Should I be afraid?"

"It's not scary. Well, perhaps a little scary." He should just say it. "Those calls and meetings you asked me about?"

"Business research."

"Sort of." He blew out a breath. "Not really. I've kept a secret from you and my family."

"O-kay." She sounded wary.

"It's better than okay. I won."

Her mouth slanted. "Won?"

"The lottery in September. Seven hundred million dollars."

Her mouth gaped. "Who knows?"

"Only you and my team who are helping me behind the scenes. It's complicated, but keeping it secret was the best way for me to provide for my family and keep them safe. The money will be collected anonymously next week. I'm sorry for not telling you."

"You had your reasons."

"You're not upset?"

"I'm thrilled for you and your family. This is the best kind of secret." She tilted her head before inhaling sharply. "You!"

"What?"

Affection filled her eyes. "You pledged the twenty-five-thousand-dollar donation to my mom's rescue."

He smiled but said nothing.

She shook her head. "Your sheepish grin is my answer."

Michael shrugged.

Sheridan touched his face. "Why did you do that?"

"Because animal rescue is important to you. I wanted to make sure the one here met their fundraising goal and your mom would have extra in January."

Sheridan threw her arms around him. "You're one of a kind."

He held her. "Thanks, but I'm just me."

"That's all you need to be."

"Once the money is deposited, let's take off. Visit galleries in Europe. Put a little distance between South Carolina and me until people lose interest in who won." He kissed her head. "What do you say?"

"I'd love to put some distance between Berry Lake and me, so I'm game. But we don't have to go to Europe. You don't have to spend a penny on me. I only want to be with you."

Her sincere tone told him she meant it. "I want you to teach me about art, so Europe will be a good place to start."

"One of the best," she agreed. "So, what happens next?"

"I can't wait to show you, because there's enough money to make all your dreams come true."

Sheridan laughed. "Then save your winnings because no spending is required."

His forehead creased. "Why?"

"You're my dream." She leaned into him. "Everything else is extra."

His face brightened. "Have I told you how much I love you?"

"A few minutes ago." She grinned. "But I don't mind hearing it again because I love you."

He brushed his hand through her hair. "I thought you would freak out over the money."

"I might later, but right now…" She licked her lower lip. "I want another kiss to ring in the new year."

And so he kissed her.

Epilogue

Summer...

At his parents' house in Charleston, Michael changed his shirt for the third time. A good thing he'd brought his largest suitcase. Tomorrow, he and Sheridan would be off on another adventure after spending a month in South Carolina to attend Hope and Josh's wedding and then Marley and Von's a few weeks later. This trip, they were flying to Japan. She wanted to see an exhibit at the art museum in Yokohama. He would enjoy the sushi and other Japanese cuisine.

As he did the buttons, his fingers trembled.

No reason to be nervous.

Except that his future happiness depended upon what happened this afternoon.

He blew out a breath.

Even now that he could afford top-of-the-line clothes, he still preferred comfort to style. But he wanted to look his best for Sheridan today. Despite the air-conditioning, he sweated. Typical for the humid summers around here, but this had more to do with his nerves than the hot temperatures outside.

It won't be long.

A knock sounded at his door. "Are you ready, Mikey?"

He adjusted his collar. "Almost."

"We need to leave in five minutes."

"Okay." His voice came across stronger than he felt. "Be right there."

The amount of money he'd won shocked his family. They'd been upset about him keeping it a secret until he told them about his team and how he'd done this to make their lives easier and keep everyone, especially Monroe and any future kiddos, safe. His family met with the lawyers and financial advisors to understand how the trust worked and the need to keep this quiet. No one, not in-laws or friends, could know, or all the steps Michael had taken would be for nothing. Mortgages and bills had been paid off, but no one had made any lifestyle changes, much to his surprise. Marley and Von had even decided to go forward with their small wedding at home. But then again, this was why Michael loved his family.

As he brushed his hand through his still-damp hair, he glanced around the bedroom full of trophies, ribbons, and awards he'd won growing up. The posters of his favorite athletes and bands—pretty much everything in here—represented a different time in his life, but he'd wanted to sleep here last night because after so many changes this year, he would make another—the best and the biggest one—today.

As long as she says yes.

She would say yes.

If she didn't, it would totally ruin the trip to Japan.

Stop thinking and finish getting dressed.

Michael checked his pocket to make sure he had what he needed before walking to the living room. Only his parents were there. His muscles bunched.

Uh-oh. His siblings and their spouses were part of this. His gut twisted. "Where is everyone else?"

"They're on their way or in Indigo Bay." His mom smiled. "No one wants Sheridan to think something's going on."

"Oh, okay." But that didn't ease the flutters in his stomach.

His father touched his shoulder. "Everything's going according to plan."

Michael nodded. "I want everything to be perfect."

His mom laughed. "Oh, sweetie. It's been perfect since the two of you decided to be boyfriend and girlfriend. This is the cherry on top. No matter what you do or say, Sheridan will be thrilled. You didn't have to go to so much trouble."

"Yes, I did, because she deserves it."

"She does, son." His dad's keys jingled. "Let's go."

Michael counted down the miles until they reached Indigo Bay. He blew out a breath. Now, the hard part began. He wiped his hands on his pants. "You know what to do."

His dad double-parked in front of the High Tide Gallery. "Yes."

"Everyone will be in place," his mom added. "You'd better hurry so you're not late."

With a nod, Michael patted his pocket to make sure he had everything he needed. "Wish me luck."

His mom shook her head. "Good luck, but you don't need it."

With that, Michael exited the car and hurried into the gallery. All he had to do was wait for Sheridan to arrive.

* * *

Sheridan walked with Hope toward the High Tide Gallery. "I don't know where Michael is, but I'm sure he'll be here when he can."

"His parents might be running behind."

They were usually prompt, but it had been a wild time with Marley and Von's wedding last week. They held the intimate ceremony and reception at the beach cottage. Simple, but it had been as beautiful as Hope and Josh's wedding at the Indigo Bay Cottages' Resort.

"So, where are you off to next?" Hope asked.

"Japan." Sheridan half laughed. "This past month is the longest we've stayed in one place since December. It's been nice, but a little weird not living out of a suitcase."

"Do you enjoy the travel?"

"I love it. Michael and I have been all over Europe and had so much fun."

Hope smiled. "I wish you could have been in Berry Lake for my gallery showing."

"My mom said you sold out. And that's where Josh proposed, right?"

"Next to the Sasquatch statue."

"That's perfect, and now you'll be part of Berry Lake Bigfoot lore."

Hope stumbled. She stuck out her arms. "A good thing I didn't fall."

"Let's slow down. We can't have the star of the exhibit bruised and scraped."

They reached the High Tide Gallery a few minutes later. A Private Event placard hung on the door.

Sheridan got chills. "Thanks for inviting us to see the show before the public arrives. One thing I miss about working at a gallery is the sneak preview."

She hadn't returned to Berry Lake. Her mom understood Sheridan needing a break and her desire to travel. Sal had never tried to contact her again. It no longer hurt as much, and the next trip after Asia would be to her hometown in September to introduce Michael to her mom.

"Are you ready?" Hope asked.

"I should ask *you*." Sheridan pulled open the door, eager to see Hope's newest works. "After you."

When Sheridan entered, she didn't see Melanie, but the dim lighting gave the interior a more intimate atmosphere. Bottles of champagne sat in a large bucket of ice. Nearby, flutes awaited the bubbly. "Fancy."

"Only the best for tonight."

"With that attitude, you'll for sure sell out." Sheridan glanced around. "Where should I start?"

"The wall over here," Hope said. "The first painting in the collection is closest to us."

Sheridan headed toward the series of works displayed together. Halfway there, she stopped.

"Oh, it's Indigo Bay. How perfect." This was where she'd met Michael, and she would always carry a piece of this town in her heart. He'd mentioned buying a place here if they didn't buy a house in Charleston. He would probably want this series. They'd been collecting art wherever they traveled. She claimed Michael spoiled her, but he said she did the same to him, so they were even. In a storage facility in Charleston, all their purchases were waiting for them when they decided not to travel as much.

She moved closer to the first one. "It's your cottage with Christmas lights on it."

The next painting showed a couple decorating a tree. She laughed. "This is what Michael and I did in December. The detail is amazing."

"You like them?" Hope asked.

"Love them. Some of your best work."

Hope beamed. "That makes me so happy to hear."

"But I thought you spent your first Christmas with Josh in Berry Lake."

"We did."

Sheridan studied the painting. "This isn't the two of you?"

"No, another couple head over heels in love."

The next work showed a proposal. The love in each stroke took Sheridan's breath away. "You nailed the detail," She squinted. Funny, but the couple kind of resembled her and Michael. She shook the thought from her head. "They're stunning. I love each one."

"And I love you, Sheridan DeMarco," Michael said from behind her.

She glanced over her shoulder.

Michael was on his knee and held a ring box out to her. Behind him, his family and hers, including Max and his daughters, stood in a half circle.

Sheridan's heart slammed against her rib cage. She faced him and everyone else. "My family is here."

"I flew them in." They'd told people he'd made his money thanks to a smart investment. No one would ever find out it was a two-dollar lottery ticket.

"But—"

"Let him talk, Sheridan," her mother urged.

In a state of shock, Sheridan nodded. "Go on."

Michael laughed. "Ever since I met you, Sheridan DeMarco, I haven't stopped thinking about you, and I wouldn't have it any other way. You're everything I didn't know I needed. I'm so glad you didn't write me off as an overgrown frat guy, because our time together has been the best adventure, and I can't wait to find out what happens next. Will you marry me?"

Her hand covered her pounding heart, and she struggled to breathe.

"Yes." She blinked, but happy tears still fell. Joy overflowed. "I want nothing more than to marry you. I love you."

Michael stood and placed the ring on her finger—a perfect fit. "I love you."

He wrapped his arms around her and kissed her.

People clapped.

"I forgot we had an audience," she whispered.

"Ignore them." He kissed her again. "Do you like the paintings?"

As she glanced at the collection on the wall, she wiped the tears off her face. "I love them."

"They're yours. Ours."

She gasped. "What?"

"Mikey commissioned them," Hope said.

"Michael," he corrected. "That'll look better on the wedding invitations."

"Wedding," Sheridan repeated. "We have to plan a wedding."

He ran his finger along her jawline. "I want to get married in Berry Lake."

"But your entire family is here." Besides, with the money he'd won, the wedding could be anywhere in the world.

"Your family and friends are there, and so are all the animals your mom cares for. This will be easier on her." He leaned his forehead against Sheridan's. "And getting married in your hometown will give you wonderful memories to replace any bad ones."

Her heart swelled with love for this man. "I love you."

And no matter where they said "I do" to each other, she knew in her heart of hearts they would live happily ever after.

* * * * *

Ready for another fun Indigo Bay Christmas Romance? Find out what happens when a matchmaker meets a local teacher in a holiday mix-up in *Sweet Mistletoe* by Elizabeth Bromke!

If you want more of Sheridan and Michael, they make an appearance in *Cupcakes & Crumbs*, the first book in my new Berry Lake Cupcake Posse series!

If you missed any of my stories featuring Marley and Von, Hope and Josh, Lizzy and Mitch, Jenny and Dare, in my Beach Brides/Indigo Bay miniseries, you can find them on my website: here www.melissamcclone.com/books/indigo-bay-series.

DID YOU MISS ONE?

Indigo Bay Christmas Romances
Sweet Tidings (Book 1) by Jean C. Gordon
Sweet Noel (Book 2) by Jeanette Lewis
Sweet Joymaker (Book 3) by Jean Oram
Sweet Yuletide (Book 4) by Melissa McClone
Sweet Mistletoe (Book 5) by Elizabeth Bromke
Sweet Carol (Book 6) by Shanae Johnson

Indigo Bay Second Chance Romances
Sweet Troublemaker (Book 1) by Jean Oram
Sweet Do-Over (Book 2) by Melissa McClone
Sweet Horizons (Book 3) by Jean C. Gordon
Sweet Complications (Book 4) by Stacy Claflin
Sweet Whispers (Book 5) by Jeanette Lewis
Sweet Adventure (Book 6) by Tamie Dearen

Indigo Bay Sweet Romance Series
Sweet Dreams (Book 1) by Stacy Claflin
Sweet Matchmaker (Book 2) by Jean Oram
Sweet Sunrise (Book 3) by Kay Correll
Sweet Illusions (Book 4) by Jeanette Lewis
Sweet Regrets (Book 5) by Jennifer Peel
Sweet Rendezvous (Book 6) by Danielle Stewart
Sweet Saturdays (Book 7) by Pamela Kelley
Sweet Beginnings (Book 8) by Melissa McClone

Sweet Starlight (Book 9) by Kay Correll
Sweet Forgiveness (Book 10) by Jean Oram
Sweet Reunion (Book 11) by Stacy Claflin
Sweet Entanglement (Book 12) by Jean C. Gordon

Holiday Short Reads
Sweet Holiday Surprise by Jean Oram
Sweet Holiday Memories by Kay Correll
Sweet Holiday Wishes by Melissa McClone
Sweet Holiday Traditions by Danielle Stewart

Missing some books from your collection?

Find out more about Indigo Bay at
www.sweetreadbooks.com/indigo-bay

ABOUT THE AUTHOR

USA Today bestselling author Melissa McClone has written over forty-five sweet contemporary romance novels. She lives in the Pacific Northwest with her husband, three children, a spoiled Norwegian Elkhound, and cats who think they rule the house. They do!

If you'd like to find Melissa online:
www.melissamcclone.com
www.facebook.com/melissamcclonebooks
www.facebook.com/groups/McCloneTroopers

OTHER BOOKS BY MELISSA MCCLONE

All series stories are standalone,
but past characters may reappear.

The Beach Brides/Indigo Bay Miniseries
A miniseries and prequel to the
Berry Lake Cupcake Posse series.
Jenny
Sweet Holiday Wishes
Sweet Beginnings
Sweet Do-Over
Sweet Yuletide

Mountain Rescue Series
Finding love in Hood Hamlet with
a little help from Christmas magic...
His Christmas Wish
Her Christmas Secret
Her Christmas Kiss
His Second Chance
His Christmas Family

One Night to Forever Series
Can one night change your life...
and your relationship status?
Fiancé for the Night
The Wedding Lullaby
A Little Bit Engaged
Love on the Slopes
The One Night To Forever Box Set: Books 1-4

The Billionaires of Silicon Forest
Who will be the last single man standing?
The Wife Finder
The Wish Maker
The Deal Breaker

Her Royal Duty
Royal romances with charming princes
and dreamy castles...
The Reluctant Princess
The Not-So-Proper Princess
The Proper Princess

Quinn Valley Ranch
Two books featuring siblings
in a multi-author series...
Carter's Cowgirl
Summer Serenade
Quinn Valley Ranch Two Book Set

A Keeper Series
These men know what they want,
and love isn't on their list.
But what happens when each meets a keeper?
The Groom
The Soccer Star
The Boss
The Husband
The Date
The Tycoon

For the complete list of books, go to:
www.melissamcclone.com/books.com

Made in the USA
Middletown, DE
24 November 2020